M000072919

KELLY RUEHLE

Saving Olivia

HOW FAR WOULD YOU GO TO SAVE A LIFE?

Preface

"Saving Olivia" is inspired by real lives and actual events. It started with evil brother's who destroyed a beautiful farm while curious sisters disappeared after they promised to save Olivia. I reluctantly became involved after receiving a desperate plea for help from two brave girls who risked everything to rescue Olivia.

There are always dark secrets lurking and a good storyteller exposes them. I began writing this story to bring awareness to the needless suffering and necessity for rescue. But I never imagined secrets being uncovered or the fate of one horse changing the lives of so many. "Saving Olivia" evolved as a saga about a little horse's rescue into stories of overcoming adversity, surviving bullying and discovering a destiny.

"Saving Olivia" is an introduction for some to the world of rescuers and the hardship and sometimes danger they face when saving a life. The Characters are inspired by real people but some of the names and places in this story have been changed to protect and respect the privacy of others.

With my hands on the wheel and my co-pilot in place, I patted Olivia's picture and said *"I got you!"*

I've written for several online and print publications. I am a writing contributor for *Bella Grace* magazine and you can follow life on the farm at Fanciful Farming on Facebook and Instagram.

Prologue

I believe we are born with a mark. A mark to be left on this world after we are gone, our "purpose". Like a distant wisp it taunts us into submission, whispering "come and find me." It can take a lifetime chasing, trying to capture that whisper. But when you do finally find it, you find peace.

Sometimes this purpose changes as we get older. Sometimes it stays the same. Many of us find it in school, we discover what we are good at and dive right in and never look back. Sometimes we follow in our parents' footsteps and other times it is found through tragedy.

I found mine through tragedy....

I love the rain, the way it smells, the way it sounds and the way it washes away and renews. But on this particular day the rain was coming down so hard it hurt my skin.

I cupped the tiny wet caterpillar in my hands. I whispered to it *"I couldn't save her, but I can save you."* It trembled slightly in my fingers. It's imperfect yellow, white and black striped body still drenched from the pouring rain. It had been knocked from the safety of its milkweed and was being washed away by the rain-formed stream that now flowed through the long grass.

As I cradled the tiny creature in that rain storm, I remembered a story I once heard long before. It talked of the spirits of our loved ones living on as a monarch butterfly after they had died. I had just lost someone I loved dearly. I lost a piece of myself when she died, I had lost my purpose too.

Could this caterpillar be MY little butterfly? To live on and be free. Could I in a sense still save her?

As a busy young adult I still found time to take walks in the woods. Still foraging for morels, wild berries, antler sheds and desperately trying to teach my young daughters to love nature as I did. They were growing up in a totally different era than me, full of intangible distractions like snapchat and instagram.

It had been many years since I had seen a monarch caterpillar I thought to myself. They were a rare sighting now. My childhood memories sprang back to a time when monarch butterflies were often seen and admired in my grandmother's garden blithely fluttering about sipping nectar. I can still picture my grandmother out there, hose in hand, watering the flowers. Her thong sandals snapping her heels as she walked. But as a young adult I couldn't recall the last time I had seen one.

I decided in that cold rain that I would take the tiny creature home with me. I worried she would once again slip from the milkweed and be swept away for good next time. I felt responsible for her.

She regained strength from her near death experience and grew quickly until one day transforming in an amazing and enchanting way. It was the most mesmerizing shade of green I had ever seen. A color you just want to surround yourself with. Garnished with gold leafing, it shined like a tiny jewel in the sunlight. So beautiful I wanted to wear it around my neck; fastened with a gold chain.

As time passed her chrysalis darkened until it became a transparent window. And then it happened, she emerged. Crinkled and shivering she perched on her now empty vessel and began to slowly open and close her wings. By late afternoon our time together had come to an end. She was ready. Her freshly dried wings opening and closing more quickly now. I held out my hand for her to crawl up on. She steadied herself and vibrated with excitement. I cradled her carefully with cupped hands outdoors.

The sun was bright that day and the air smelled like fresh tree blossoms. I opened my hands and she crawled to the tips of my fingers, staring out into her new world. She remained still for several seconds just taking it all in. Then, she tapped her wings together and let go. I thanked her for helping me to heal my heart and allowing me to find my purpose again; I thought I had lost my purpose only to find it again in a different way. I had rescued a tiny life and watched it fly blissfully off into the sunlight. I now wanted to rescue others, heal them, take away their sadness and show them what I had learned.. that we all have a purpose no matter what.

Like the caterpillar transforming into a monarch butterfly, Fanciful Farm made its own transformation from being a beautiful and small hobby farm with gardens of lavender, fruiting shrubs, buzzing bees, lovely chickens and show quality horses to a sanctuary for the hurt and broken hearted.

We all seek to leave our mark on this earth before we are gone and this is our mark.

Fanciful Farm is a four generation run family hobby farm inspired by those we have loved and lost. We promote compassion and love to all of mother nature's creations. Fanciful Farm strives to work with nature, not against it in a harmonious balance. Along the way teaching our youngest generation of farmers that the wonders of nature is our greatest gift of all. -Danielle Raad

© Kelly Ruehle 2020

ISBN: 978-1-09830-044-9

eBook ISBN: 978-1-09830-045-6

All rights reserved. This book or any portion thereof may not be reproduced or used in any manner whatsoever without the express written permission of the publisher except for the use of brief quotations in a book review.

Saving Olivia

"What do you want?" I asked.
"To live," she said.

Olivia after her hair grew back with my granddaughter Giselle

The Farm

"

Yesterday, I caught a whiff of something familiar. The scent awoke a memory that ached and trembled inside my chest. I wasn't sure if it had been provoked by damp earth clinging to a rock from my latest trip or the warm breeze licking the back of my neck.

I looked over at Olivia, completely unaware that I was about to relive her past.

"

All night I wished for morning but it felt like it would never come. I tossed and turned until the alarm gave me permission to leave my bed. I should have been tired, exhausted actually but the high of an addict was still very much alive in my head. Saving something from the brink of death or worse - a lifetime of suffering was addictive and easily got out of hand. My living, breathing collection was growing every time a new save enticed me into action.

I've always wanted to save everything. When I was a child I thought I could. The first time I realized that I was as small as a tiny grain of sand and totally unable to save everything and everyone happened while walking the beach.

I remember that I was struck by the way they were meticulously lined up across the sand. Momma's flip flops, daddy's tennis shoes and baby's tiny slip ons nestled safely between. I stood and admired the perfect little family of shoes. I thought about snapping a picture until a distant glance caught my attention. I smiled at the young woman who caught me eyeing her lovely display. I started to comment on the cute I found in this artful arrangement. But something forced my lips to tighten and my voice to seize. It was this moment that I knew. I knew by the way her eyes met mine, deep and penetrating. It was evident in the way her face fell paralyzed over the family of shoes; each one tightly pressed against one another. The larger shoes quietly protected the tiny shoes in the center.

Somehow I knew, even before I noticed that the barefoot family sitting in the sand was a family of two instead of three. The little feet belonging to the tiny shoes were nowhere in sight. My eyes looked away in discomfort at first but within seconds I braved the discomfort and searched the young woman's face until our eyes met again. An understanding was exchanged without words. This perfect display of shoes presented a precious memory. Our thoughts mingled and our hearts pinged. Then suddenly the tear sliding down her cheek became mine. A smile was inappropriate and words were unnecessary when we parted ways. One tiny wink later I turned and walked on down the beach with a piece of that young mother's heart tucked into mine. I turned back to steal a quick glance of the empty shoes just one more time.

I felt each grain of sand a little sharper now slipping beneath my feet. The salty breeze dried the tears that flowed down my cheeks. The sun was warm and comforting on my back while the memory of the empty little shoes became etched in my mind. I smiled for the borrowed memory of a child I never met, graciously shared by a mother who will never forget.

It was early on that brisk September day when I rushed my morning routine and left the house in a hurry. I carried my halogen flashlight while the dark sky was begging the sun to rise. The moment my foot touched the grass an eerie sound echoed through the trees, sending a shiver up my spine. It was the sound of a barred owl perched in the old hickory overlooking my well-worn path. A little startled, I stopped for a few minutes and waited for the moon to fall below the horizon, allowing the morning sun to guide my way. There was a slight nip in the air so I reached in my pocket and pulled on my wool cap, before completing my walk down the woodland trail. Although my routine was the same, something had changed.

The long trip, the late hours and my new responsibility made my head heavy with worry and cloudy from lack of sleep. I was anxious about the day ahead and after a deep breath or two the fluttery dance in my chest settled into a slow waltz. I reminded my worried self that all of the extra anxiety was unwarranted but couldn't shake the uneasy feeling bubbling from my belly to my chest. My fingers brushed through my hair, twirling a lock into the perfect spiral down my forehead. This was a habit turned ritual, practiced whenever my nerves were on high alert. I fretted because there hadn't been enough time to get the new cameras up in the barn and I could only hope and pray that all had gone well overnight. I reassured myself that everything was okay and there was nothing to be worried about. My worry wart tendencies weren't earned but inherited from generations of women who obsessed over each bump and bruise and every fever, anything real or imagined that their children may or may not have suffered.

The welcome sight of my big red barn came into view when I rounded the corner. A familiar smell of cedarwood, horse manure and lavender filled my senses and brought a smile to my face. I placed my hand on the door to the barn and mumbled the words, *"you're ready for whatever this day may bring."* It was busy and loud when I walked through the door. The chickens squawked, the goats wrestled, and the horses nayed for breakfast. This wasn't unusual as most of my mornings began this way. I wasted no time with a wellness check as I opened each and every stall. My little horse "Mimi" who was smaller than a Labrador retriever ran up to me and shook my pants with her teeth. This was her way of letting me know she was ready for breakfast. I knelt down on one knee and scratched Mimi between the ears. *"Have patience with me little girl."* Before I had risen to my feet her stall-mate Sully brushed up against my thigh in reminder of his presence. I peeked in on Chip and then Olivia as I completed the wellness checks of my special needs horses before moving on to the minis who enjoyed life without difficulty or handicap. The barn, although chaotic at times, was the best way to start and my favorite place to end a long day.

I chose this life after many years of participating in the normal hustle while commuting through traffic and sitting at a desk for over eight hours each day. For most of my adult life I had been searching for something more meaningful and personal and I'd finally found it. As a child my favorite things were animals and my grandparents farm. I loved walking through grandpa's garden and the way it felt to swing back and forth on the rope that hung from the loft of the barn. This was my special place where I had spent hours imagining it's past as a working farm with busy hands tending the animals. I cherished all my memories of the old farm but the one that danced most vividly in my mind was the scent of fresh linens that lingered about the clothesline as I ran my fingers through the softness of my grandmother's fluffy white sheets. That's when I knew that someday

I would live there too and bring the old farm back to the picturesque scene that lived in my head. I imagined Betsy the cow wandering the pasture with a bell dangling about her neck. The charm of it all made me long for my own farm. I never worried about how or when it would happen because I was a child and still believed. All through my adult life the images of my little farm begged until that dream merged with my reality. Although my grandparents' farm has long faded into my past, I no longer needed to pretend while feeding the chickens.

Farms are a lot of work with many hours spent keeping each animal happy and healthy. The farm that I built was much different than my grandparents' farm. In an effort to recreate the images of a simple family farm I had gone a little too far. What I created was anything but simple. It was complicated like me with double the worry and maybe even triple the maintenance and responsibilities. Herb gardens, honey bees, a monarch butterfly sanctuary, farmers markets, milking goats, exotic chickens and miniature horses; many fragile with special needs filled the space and occupied almost every waking moment of my life. The dishes, laundry and house cleaning had to wait for the farm chores to be done. I had pulled my husband into this daunting responsibility by telling him *"remember you said you always wanted a farm."* I don't think this is quite what he had in mind when he thought about becoming a farmer. I sometimes felt guilty over the extra burden placed on my family, especially my husband, caring for the farm, physically and financially. But somehow my guilt never stopped me. Although my farm was complicated and a little over the top, I loved every minute spent there. My goats were rowdy and sometimes difficult to manage but usually healthy. My chickens were easy to manage but their health was challenging at times. We ran a no-kill farm which allowed the animals to live out their days until disease or old age got the best of them. Some had short life spans and the aging process wasn't easy for a chicken. But the horses were my most cherished and challenging project of all. Many of the equine residents on this farm were rescues with special needs and they suffered from significant health issues. Although it was difficult and expensive to tend to every ailment, this work was important and it had my heart.

Every animal was standing eagerly awaiting their breakfast and my nervousness from that morning dissipated once I began the daily chores. After I prepared the rubber bowls with a scoop of grain, I collected the freshly laid green and brown speckled eggs. I was amazed at the beauty and perfection of each when I carefully removed them from my apron pockets one by one. After inspection, I placed them in the egg basket resting on an old white dresser inside the barn. As I removed the last egg from my apron, I noticed something strange in the dark shadows of a nearby stall. Something had happened within the brief time I was in the chicken coop collecting the eggs.

I was afraid to move closer. Afraid to see what I had feared all morning. My head was swimming as I took a deep breath and willed myself to put one foot in front of the other. Everything fell silent except my heart pounding like a drum within my ears. I looked into the stall and saw a dark form moving along the floor. It was as if a hand had reached up and grabbed me by the throat when I recognized Olivia lying in the corner of her stall, rocking back-and-forth. I gasped and the perfectly formed egg fell from my hand to the concrete floor below. When it smashed to the unforgiving ground, a golden yolk spilled out in front of me. I quickly turned my attention to Olivia, lying helplessly on the cold floor. I covered my lips with my hand to stifle a scream as I knelt over Olivia's quivering body. My body crumpled to the floor, devastated and unable to get up because I knew that my worst fears had come true. This meant that things had changed and nothing would ever be the same. A dream, a plan, and a life was over; wasted just like the shattered egg that lay at my feet. Finally a scream left my lips and every animal in the barn fell silent to listen.

· · · · · ● · · · ·

Before going any deeper into the devastating events that ran my mouth dry, making it almost impossible to swallow the hard lump stuck in the back of my throat, I fluttered back to how this heartbreak got started. It began long before Olivia came to live in my barn. It was hard to know exactly where to start. I closed my eyes and returned to the beginning where I said, " *I looked over at Olivia, completely unaware that I was about to relive her past.*"

For me, it all began when I received a frantic call asking for my help with a little horse who was in desperate need. After the call I asked myself, "do you really have the time and money to take on a new project?" I wasn't sure that I could handle another difficult case but how could I have turned my back on a friend and refused to help. A nagging voice had told me that the call happened for a reason and Olivia was meant to live on my farm. I felt compelled to take on the responsibility. That voice in my head begged and pleaded for my help and this began a nagging conversation between the voice and my good sense. But once I placed good sense aside, the voice that remained planned the mission and I was on my way to save Olivia.

Although my part of the story had begun with the pleading phone call, Olivia's story started long before. A breeze blew past my tear stained cheeks as the words tumbled down from the sky. This is Olivia's story, told the best way I know how.

Her journey began in a place I had never seen. This place was home to many innocent souls plagued by unspeakable secrets that they themselves could never tell. The ugly truth was whispered to the masked graves of the horses who lost the battle before the cavalry came. A breathless shudder came over me whenever I thought of it.

Before this little horse came to my farm she was a miniature horse living on a big farm overrun with little horses. The farm had been affectionately called Sadie's Farm by the locals. Sadie's family owned the property for generations, but it was she who brought the farm to life. Sadie left her mark and inspirational beauty with sweeping pastures, immaculate barns and lovely horses running throughout. She loved that farm and it showed. Although Sadie's name was still used when referencing the property, times changed and hardship had caused her to lose the farm.

Sadie's Farm was located in the deep south at the foot of the beautiful Appalachians, just outside a quaint little village of less than six hundred people. The village had been settled by hard working folks who knew their neighbors and took pride in their properties until the economy changed, the factory closed and the residents fell on hard times. The sturdy roots of the community had begun to rot away which left the fallen debris of poverty and addiction. Hardship eventually reached the little horse farm at the base of the mountain. At one time, this farm, framed by lovely mountains and drenched in the ambiance of running horses, had been a wonderful place to live. But once Sadie lost the farm, that description couldn't be further from the truth. In a perfect world people were always kind to one another, properties were immaculately kept, and their animals were cherished and loved forever but that perfection was far, far away from Sadie's farm. This perfect world is a fallacy placed in the minds of well-meaning people and I have never seen a world so perfect.

Olivia

"

Strength isn't necessary in the flesh
but required in the mind

"

We are all born into circumstances beyond our control. While some may inherit good fortune, warm hearts and full bellies; others live in squalid conditions without proper care. But then there are those who seem to have everything they need. The outside looks good, a pretty package wrapped neatly in the perfect bow, hiding the broken pieces, shattered by rough handling and lack of care. The damage stays hidden, unnoticed and undiscovered until the moment the package is unwrapped. Don't judge a book by it's cover, beauty is only skin deep and looks are deceiving would all apply to Olivia's secrets that went unnoticed and undiscovered until the bow came undone and the contents were exposed.

Olivia's life began in a land flanked by lovely mountains and southern breezes. She was part of a ruse, on a run down farm with a reputation for turning out well-bred horses. The farm owners made a hobby of collecting horses they could sell at a higher price. This deceitful ploy had been driven by greedy men without a conscience. Their alive, kicking, flesh and blood meant nothing. The horses were just a commodity that turned a profit or found a grave. Life on the farm was lonely and every horse was desperate. Like a Carousel going around and around in an endless cycle, Olivia and the other horses were on a never ending ride with no way to escape. Desperate for love, desperate for security and desperate for food. The lie began with a picturesque view that lured you in, the flaws were eased by distance but the close-up was met with bitter disappointment. Olivia was born in the early spring that quickly turned into summer while she was fed and protected by her mother. When she was only a few months old, her mother and several other horses were taken to auction and sold to the highest bidder. Olivia whinnied as she watched her mother being led up the ramp and into a dark trailer filled with other horses. The horses were loud in protest as her mother was stuffed into the already congested space. Olivia was unaware of what was happening to her mother but she knew it wasn't good and looked with tearful eyes and confusion when the door closed and the trailer left the farm. She heard her mother whinny as the trailer disappeared from her sight. That day changed her life forever and ended the days of mercy for Olivia.

Fear began its slow crawl up Olivia's spine when she stood alone for the first time. She looked around the pasture and worried about where to go. Her mother always led the way and protected her when it was time to eat, time to rest and time to stand up to the unruly herd. Once her protection was gone the bullies in the herd turned on Olivia with fear and vengeance in their eyes. After the horses grew tired of bullying Olivia she tucked herself beneath a giant tree and waited for her mother to return.

An idyllic life running through green pastures wasn't part of her reality. But Olivia sometimes dreamed of beautiful green grasses. Her dreams continued with legs that were able to run with the herd like a normal horse. It ended with a full belly that never felt the pains of hunger. The reality of Olivia's condition was far different than what she dreamed about. The ground beneath her feet was brown and muddy, filled with ruts and absent of grass. This unfortunately made life difficult for Olivia. It was impossible for her unorthodox body to run or even walk like the other horses. Olivia was born different, she was kicked, bitten and chased until her legs buckled. She worked hard to avoid the horses who were desperate and became bullies. Olivia struggled to survive while a fire burned in her hollow belly. There was barely enough food to keep the herd alive and Olivia was ranked at the bottom, which meant she ate last.

Her body became frail and her hair was falling out, each day became more challenging than the last. Olivia knew she had to fight for her life because she saw what happened to those who had given up. They vanished from sight, ashes and dust beneath her feet. Olivia's mother never returned. She fended for herself without a mother or a friend making sure she was safe and well fed. The other horses didn't care if Olivia had enough to eat because they were starving and fought over what little food they had. But when Olivia looked into their eyes, she didn't see evil, just fear and desperation. When cornered, scared and hungry they reverted to their instincts. They hadn't intentionally hurt her. Their violent behavior was merely a horrible by-product of survival.

The entire herd suffered the same pains, but her disabilities made it harder. Olivia was born with a body that didn't fit together as it should. When looking at Olivia it was obvious that her front legs were shorter than her back legs and her shoulders were frozen in place. This odd deformity caused friction when her bones rubbed together which forced them to become stiff, fused together. Olivia's body swayed about the pasture with a serpent-like motion, swinging her head from side to side. She survived even though she was no match for the horses who bullied and chased her. She learned early on to stay hidden and quietly watched the other horses eat. But after they walked away, Olivia moved in to clean up the crumbs they had left behind. When there wasn't enough leftover hay to eat, she foraged on roots and leaves to get by. Olivia felt her life slipping every time a clump of her hair left her body and floated to the ground, disappearing into the moist earth at her feet.

Olivia lived in constant fear of the other horses. But she was most afraid of the brothers who ran the farm, especially when they opened the gate and eyed the pasture. Nothing good ever came to a horse who was chosen and she was determined to become invisible. The hands that worked the farm had been unkind, their hollow eyes were mean and hard as rocks. The wicked farm owners were brothers. The brothers acquired the farm on a greedy whim at auction during a tax deed sale. Despite the fact that they were chronically unemployed and frequently drunk. The brothers grew up poor in a broken family without a father. The men who frequently spent the night with their mother were often abusive to the boys. This forced them to leave the trailer they shared with their mother and find their own way at an early age. The Johnson brothers took a job at the local mill and made enough money to support themselves until the recession hit. Once the mill and local factory closed, jobs were hard to come by. The brothers turned to alcohol and petty theft. They conned elderly people out of their life savings with promises to replace a roof or fix the furnace. The jobs were never completed and the brothers took payment up front. Once they had saved enough money to buy some property the Johnson boys placed a bid on silent auction and bought the farm. This was the worst possible outcome for Sadie's Farm. But Sadie had no claim to the farm or her horses anymore and could only walk away in shame. The brothers were mean but only grew more evil with the overwhelming responsibilities and constant frustrations of owning a horse farm. The meanest and worst of the Johnson brothers was the short squatty man with a red face and a large vein that pulsed from his shiny head when he was angry. He snapped a whip across Olivia's legs when she moved too slowly. She felt the stinging pain and the blood falling from her open wounds that eventually became deep scars.

The evil brother's greed was beyond anything Sadie could have imagined. Lucky for her she had moved away shortly after losing the farm. Sadie wouldn't have survived knowing about the evil that took over her lovely home. When the brothers attempts to profit from the usual sale of horses failed, they began to use the slaughterhouses for a way to make ends meet. Every year over 100,000 American horses are transported to Canada and Mexico to be slaughtered and their meat shipped to Europe for human consumption. Horse meat is viewed as a delicacy in Europe costing around $20 per pound. Horse meat in America is considered taboo. Horses are normally considered pets in America and it is taboo to eat its meat. The Johnson brothers didn't worry about cruelty and they certainly didn't care if their actions were considered taboo.

Olivia tried to stay small and out of sight in fear that she would become one of the unlucky ones, one less mouth to feed for the greedy farm owners. Olivia hid the best she could while she hoped the men forgot that she had ever existed. Every time a horse disappeared, Olivia wondered if she was next; why had she been allowed to live? She wondered what happened to the others who seemed to have evaporated into thin air. Olivia tried to stop thinking about the disappearing horses but she couldn't. Fear occupied almost every waking minute of Olivia's life. But her fears became more intense after her little friend suddenly vanished. Olivia's little friend was very young and unusually small.

The sorrel filly began following Olivia the day she crept into her hiding place under the willow tree. This young filly was tiny and frail, much smaller than the other young horses her age. It didn't take long before the little horse noticed that Olivia looked different and couldn't run like the others. But she didn't seem to mind Olivia's odd body or unusual sway. She was content to quietly keep Olivia company. Soon after they met Olivia began following her friend and learned of a promising area to graze. She began following her little friend to a spot where a few sprigs of grass had begun to grow. She and her friend munched on fresh shoots until they were gone. It was then that the little filly stood nose to nose and stared into Olivia's eyes. The little filly appeared to be lonely when she rubbed her muzzle up and down Olivia's neck. They walked single file beneath the branches while they searched the tree line for roots or fallen leaves. The filly followed along behind Olivia seemingly attached to her new friend. The young filly had found herself alone one morning after having been separated from her mother the night before. She was afraid to pass by the unruly stallion to find her. She was unaware that the stallion's aggressive behavior was protecting her from an untimely death when he held her back, away from her mother who had become one of the unlucky ones that silently disappeared into the night. The young horse missed her mother and Olivia became a trustworthy substitute. The filly entertained Olivia when she ran in circles around and around her, kicking up her heels and tripping over her tangled hooves. The filly's strawberry mane graced her neck in short little spikes that stood on end and pulsed as she ran. Time went by quickly while Olivia was distracted by her new friend. The little filly took Olivia's mind off her troubles and kept her from feeling alone. They spent several weeks together and the new friendship eased Olivia's pains of hunger.

One afternoon while Olivia was searching for new shoots to eat she realized she hadn't seen the tiny filly all day. She searched the field, under the trees and behind the barn. Olivia was worried. She took her chances when she walked in front of the barn in perfect view of the Johnson brothers' farmhouse, something Olivia had never done since it was usually met with unfortunate consequences for others who had dared. The barn was quiet and there were no signs of her tiny friend. The little filly was gone. As Olivia walked back to her safe place beneath the tree, she wondered why the tiny filly had gone missing. Although she tried to convince herself that her friend was ok, just hiding somewhere nearby and that she would show up before dark, Olivia was well aware that disappearing horses was a common occurrence that never ended well. She knew what happened even though she wished she hadn't. On her way back, Olivia tried to look straight ahead, focused on her destination under the willow tree. Her eyes were staring straight ahead until she heard a calling from the trees begging for her attention. Just one glance, one tiny second of her time was the message coming from the branches that swayed in the breeze. She tried to ignore the whispering wood but her plan to not look toward the trees was unsuccessful. She had a bad feeling and needed to know. So she did it, she looked and Olivia didn't like what she had seen - a fresh mound of earth along the tree line outside the pasture fence. Olivia noticed the stallion standing on the hill looking toward the trees with a tear in his eye. The stallion knew - Olivia knew. Her head dropped as she slipped under the low hanging branches. Her heart ached and her body felt cold and tired because Olivia knew what rotted beneath the earthy mounds. She stood under the willow alone and felt as if she had forgotten how to breathe. Olivia intentionally pushed and pulled the breath into her lungs for fear she would suffocate if she didn't. She never got used to the pain of losing a friend or her unknowing of what would happen next. The loss of her friend cut Olivia deep but she knew she had to be strong to stay alive, she tried to pretend like it never happened and like they had never met.

The horses feared the ruthless farm owners who ended the lives of those who showed little to no promise of profits. The tiny filly was fragile and much too small to contribute to the bottom line by producing offspring to sell at auction. There was no conscience, no heart and no mercy on Sadie's Farm that was now controlled by the evil Johnson brothers.

Just as she had practiced many times before, Olivia pushed the sadness down deep where it couldn't bubble up at a moments notice. It was a hard but necessary part of her survival and something Olivia did more times than she would like to remember. After several days, Olivia was comfortable, once again, in her aloneness and began to manage pretty well - except for the night. Darkness brought on different challenges. When the food was gone, but bellies were still hungry, the desperate herd became mean and nasty, lashing out when she tried to get close. When the others felt vengeful, Olivia retreated to her dark corner under the giant willow tree to wait out the night. The tree's long wispy branches were moss-hung and embraced her body in a safe haven of quiet darkness hidden from the moonlight. It was there that Olivia stood, hushed, out of sight, while she waited for the morning.

Olivia was born on this farm, it's all she had ever known but there were days that all she thought about was dying in this heartless place she was forced to call home. Several years before Olivia was born, the farm, known as Sadie's Farm by the locals, was a pleasant homestead. The moss-draped live oaks stood stern and tall along the sweeping drive to the farmhouse where they once bred beautiful horses that sold to some of the most prestigious show homes. The fields had flourished in cover crops and the little horses appreciated full bellies and kind owners. By the time Olivia was born, the fields were bare and the barn was in desperate need of repair. Money was tight and profits were the only thing that mattered to the greedy Johnson brothers.

Sadie

"

> *Salty tears are like tiny raindrops when they fall. Ordinary and unnoticed, unless they are yours - their invisibility to others doesn't make the sting any less painful.*

"

S he was fragile, a gentle old soul. Not the kind of person who would ever have intentionally brought about suffering or a catastrophe. She never meant to hurt anyone least of all her prized possessions. Her horses were like her children after they both had grown and left the nest. She had spent a life-time sitting on her porch looking out over the lush fields of green in awe of the beauty that surrounded her. She never wanted to leave.

Her home was a picturesque farmhouse with all the country touches like a big front porch with a swing and trellised perennial gardens. The butcher block counters held so many memories from her childhood; baking cookies, carving the Thanksgiving turkey and all the long talks shared over a simple cup of tea. Every part of the old house was special and she loved the way the smooth bannis-ter curved beneath her fingers. She helped plant almost every tree along the fence line. The gardens were filled with her favorite flowers like yellow jasmine, climbing roses, pink hydrangeas and her favorite magnolia tree. It smelled of honeysuckle, sweet grass and home. Many of her afternoons were spent in the garden enjoying the beautiful blooms and hedy scent. Everything about the farmhouse, her perennial gardens, the barn, the pastures and her horses smelled like home. She was born on the farm and she thought she would die there. But, somehow life, or more accurately money, had come between them, the farm, her inheritance and life as she knew it- gone forever. Losing the farm was hard for her to accept but it was even harder walking out the door knowing she would never again walk across the old wooden planks with a familiar squeak.

Sadie wondered how to leave something she had loved so much, a part of her heart and her soul. She had lost everything… her home, her horses, even her neighbors. She loved this land and the people she worshiped with, friends who held her hand when her father died and neighbors whose kids she watched grow up. She would never see Billy, the little boy next door, grown up. He was special, not right from the day he was born. He needed help that his mother couldn't give. Billy was barely old enough to visit the horses when Sadie left. She had promised his mother she would work with him, bring him over to spend time in the barn. She hoped her little horses could get through to Billy by allowing his mind to connect with something outside of himself. Sadie shook her head in frustration. *Lord knows the poor boy doesn't get any attention at home with his father gone and his mother working two jobs to put food on the table.* The last time she saw Billy she whispered a promise to him that she would help, promised herself too. But she never followed through and now it's too late. She thought she had time. She never imagined she would leave because she'd been here forever. She was so sure about her life on the farm being forever. But then she had been so sure her marriage would last too. Till death do us part meant nothing to Donny and their breakup had cost her everything; her happiness, her home, her horses.

Sadie picked up the beautiful little horse statue that Donny had presented to her on their wedding night. She twirled it around and stared as if her mind were someplace else. She remembered how happy she felt, how hers and Donny's lives were just beginning. So much time had been wasted on a dream that was now broken into a million little pieces. Then she closed her eyes and thought about her father and how proud he was of the farm. The farmhouse had meant everything to him. He helped his father build it and knew every board and every nail. It's a good thing he didn't live to see what she'd done, her failed marriage and the fact that she destroyed the farm. *What would Daddy have said?* She could almost hear the words falling from his thin lips. "Didn't I tell you that man was no good? You should have left that SOB a long time ago, found yourself a good one. Now look what ya gone and done. Ain't nobody gonna take care of this place like the Livingstons. And them horses, they be better off dead."

It forced a tear just thinking about it. Sadie placed her hands on her belly trying to squelch the ache that she knew she deserved. *It's all my fault. I shoulda known better. I've ended a lifetime of work and generations of pride. As for my horses; daddy may have been right. They probably were better off dead.* It was so true what her grandmother had said that day she graduated high school and thought about leaving the farm to live in the city, "When you're born on the farm, you take to this life naturally like breathin' and dyin'. You know the smells and the sounds of the animals, it's a safe place." Sadie pounded her fist on the porch rail and shouted, *until you can't afford to keep your head above water, then you float down the river belly up and inevitably drown.*

Sadie Livingston was a young woman with a promising life ahead of her when she started a family on her grandfather's picturesque farm at the base of the Appalachians in South Carolina. She married her husband Donald, or Donny as she called him and he became part of the farm right after the wedding. They built a beautiful life together, two kids and the horses; her beautiful little horses. Sadie cried out into the empty halls. *We were happy, really happy… until we weren't. The day the factory closed everything changed, Donny changed. He tried to find another job, he really did!* The ugly recession hit the town like a hurricane destroying everything in its path. Once Donny took to the bottle his kind demeanor evaporated and turned into someone Sadie didn't recognize. Twelve bottles of cheap beer later he became junkyard-dog-mean. Before long the money was gone, spent on booze and gambling and then three years of taxes went unpaid. Sadie had no choice, the county sold the farm. Tears, so many tears. *What would happen to my precious little horses? No one will love them like I have.* Sadie had tried desperately to uphold a promise to find a loving home with a dedicated farm owner to take care of her horses. But that promise was just like all the others; broken into tiny shattered pieces that cut through her chest with the precision of a sharp knife.

Sadie knew it was all her fault, she'd done this! She was responsible and now her children would never inherit the farm. The Livingston legacy- over and done. Her pride was gone, crushed into a million pieces and scattered on the wooden floor. Sadie thought about walking until she was waist deep in the pond and then she'd keep going until the water was over her head, rushing in her ears so she didn't have to hear the sounds of failure, the murkiness shielding her eyes so she wouldn't have to look at what she had done and eventually the cold water filling her lungs… deadly and complete. She stood and stared at the pond for a moment before walking away.

Sadie looked at the little brown horse in her hand. *This thing is of no use to me now. Just an awful reminder of Donny, my failed marriage and a life that's over.* She ran her finger down the white blaze on the nose before placing it in a box addressed to her niece Gracie May in West Virginia. With her aching head resting in her hands she vividly recalled walking through her empty farmhouse one last time. She ran her fingers along the railings and touched every door handle, while memories raw and bleeding filled her head. The days of her childhood, the night of her wedding, the birth of her children and the death of her parents. There were all those dinners around the farmhouse table that her grandfather had built and then there was the day she stood on the porch with tears in her eyes as she sent her youngest child off to college. The secrets, the laughter and the tears are now left behind in the old farmhouse without purpose, bumping into walls and falling to the floor. Locked away in this house that is no longer hers. Sadie's head felt swollen from the guilt that was eating away at her brain. She swallowed hard and tried to swat the memories away like a pesky horsefly, it was so painful to relive the past. Sadie recalled standing at the kitchen sink, looking out toward the barn one last time, her eyes burning with salty tears. But she quickly looked away before her heart crumbled into a million dusty pieces that could have floated away with the slightest breeze. When she loaded the last box into her Toyota hatchback, she swore she heard the wind whisper "you can't undo the past." She shivered when she took one last look at her farmhouse; the only place she had ever lived. This farm had been the best part of Sadie. It was under her fingernails and it weaved it's way in and out of every cell. She felt it living and breathing inside her. When she walked away from the farm, it wasn't without losing a part of herself. Flesh and blood from her insides were ripped out and they left a massive hole in her chest too big to fill. She remembered the old saying: *when one door closes another one opens.* Sadie hadn't believed it… None of the doors opening and closing had been her choice... not directly anyway. Giant elephant tears rolled down her cheeks and came to rest on her lips, salty and stinging as she drove away.

Olivia

"

A promise for the future floats on the breeze during moments of laughter, because everyone has a place and everything is on its way to somewhere, I promise.

"

Olivia was lonely when her new friends first arrived. Lonely because she was different and lonely because she wasn't a welcomed part of the herd. Olivia only wanted to be normal like the others and thought she could fake it if she tried hard enough. For a vulnerable animal, like Olivia, acting normal and fitting in was a necessary part of survival but animals aren't easily fooled. Horses have keen intuition; guided by instinct and body language. Olivia's disabilities were hard to hide, her body was a dead giveaway. Unable to fool the others, she became a loner and kept to herself. Hiding from the horses who bullied her and from the farmhands who had little patience for a crippled horse was the only way she survived. Olivia's crippled body was a fortress and she was a prisoner who became complicit with her invisibility.

Olivia knew fear all too well. It was an up close and personal part of her daily experience. The day she learned that not all people were bad was a day when two young girls paid her a visit. It was the perfect day for this to happen, after the terrible night Olivia had experienced. Just the day before a violent storm came out of the north and brought down the roof of the farmhouse. The brothers were in a foul mood when they came home and found the yard littered with debris. Olivia heard their salty language as they moved closer to the barn. She ducked under her favorite tree to avoid the cruel hands she'd experienced in the past. Olivia stayed under the tree frightened, invisible and alone all night. She listened to the drunken rage that grew louder as the night progressed. Olivia could see flickers of light slithering between the trees. Popping sounds and then loud whooshes as the flames grew higher and higher until the light towered over the trees. There were truck engines roaring, loud music blaring and wild evil laughter that echoed off each and every tree. The night lasted forever while she listened and waited. Olivia was relieved that nothing bad had happened to her and happy when the morning light came and the rest of the herd was still there. It was a very long and lonely night so Olivia was interested when the girls cheerful faces arrived the very next day.

This first encounter with two young girls, who called themselves "the spy sisters" happened because they were bored and wandering. The sisters... one redheaded, who lost her ability to speak at a young age and one blonde who was the redhead's voice and best friend did everything together. The girls poke their noses into everything and everybody's business while looking for something more interesting than what they experienced at home. The sisters had just finished the latest spy novel and they were searching for a real-life mystery of their own to solve when they wandered onto the farm and found Olivia.

This search led them down the road where they were excited to find a field overrun with little horses. The blonde sister wasn't concerned about the danger or consequences of trespassing onto a strangers' property when she begged her red headed sister to join her. After they climbed the pasture gate, the sisters skipped toward the other horses before they noticed Olivia as she stood all alone, apart from the herd. Olivia was nervous at first, unsure if they could be trusted when she saw the two young strangers headed her way. She quickly ducked beneath a long hanging canopy of trees. But, these little girls weren't discouraged by Olivia's reclusive nature. This was an invitation to the girls for fun. Instead of shying away the sisters made it a game of hide and seek which lasted most of the afternoon. Olivia refused to play along as she was sure they would grow tired of her stubbornness but in the end it was she who had given in. Olivia decided to let them win the moment the little redhead's twinkling eyes met hers. Olivia didn't know the red haired girl with the pale green eyes but she wanted to. This day was the beginning of what became a very important and lasting friendship.

Every afternoon after school, Olivia's young friends climbed over the pasture fence with a tasty snack. Some days it was an apple, others a carrot.

The food was delicious but it wasn't the best part of their visit. Olivia enjoyed their pets, soft spoken words and most of all… their affection.

The blonde sister, a precocious girl stood a little taller than her red haired sister. Her eyes were bright blue and her hair matched the sun. The redhead was small and pale with freckles and a petite little nose. Her eyes were green with a tiny fleck of gold around the edges. The redheaded sister brought a hand to her lips when she watched Olivia struggle. She winced a little as Olivia painfully drug her shaggy brown body across the dirt. The girls felt badly about Olivia's pathetic state when they pinky swore to earn her trust and become her friend. The little redhead felt a kindred spirit toward Olivia because she too was less than perfect.

Little Red knew what it felt like to be different and misunderstood by the kids at school. Her face appeared sad when the other horses were mean, chasing the crippled little horse away from the hay. Little Red had a big sister to speak up and protect her but Olivia had no one. Red had become unable to speak when she was very young. This forced her to communicate in other ways. She looked deep into Olivia's eyes and silently expressed everything she wanted to say. Olivia heard every unspoken word. She knew just how much Little Red cared. Red was especially fond of Olivia's one blue eye because it was luminous like the pale blue skies on a clear day. Little Red saw her reflection when she perfected an expression of care and concern for Olivia. She fussed with Olivia's long tail that draped across the ground and puddled at her feet. Little Red's hands were gentle when she pulled the burrs from Olivia's sun bleached fur. She then patted her head and kissed the little white swirl that graced Olivia's forehead.

It was Blondie who first decided on Olivia's name. This little horse reminded her of the young girl whose picture she'd found with the name "Olivia" written in black pen on the backside of the photo. The girl was unfamiliar to the sisters but the old Polaroid picture was in amongst their mother's things. The little girl in the picture was sitting in a wheelchair. Blondie liked the dimples on the face of this little girl with a sweet smile and a head full of wild brown hair. Neither of the sisters recognized the face of the girl in the photo as being anyone they had ever met. But for some reason this photo and the name Olivia had always felt special to Blondie. Maybe the dimpled little girl was someone their mother once knew or even cared about dearly. Blondie pulled her sparkly pink pen out of her back pocket and handed it to her sister. "Hey Red, I think we should name her Olivia after the little girl with big dimples in mama's box." Red smiled when she wrote the name "Olivia" on her sister's palm and then on her own palm she wrote the word "perfect!" with an exclamation point. They high fived. "That's it! From now on she shall be called Olivia." Blondie did a cartwheel before she took a permanent marker from her back pocket and wrote the letters; O L I V I A on the inside of the horse's ear over a bare patch of skin that had refused to grow hair. The little horse stood very still as if she had understood their words and totally trusted their actions.

Some of the sisters visits with Olivia turned into story hour. The little blonde spy read from her favorite books about super sleuths who followed the evidence and always solved the mystery while the redheaded spy braided Olivia's mane. Olivia loved being read to but preferred to hear about real life adventures instead of their storybooks. Her favorite spy sister adventure was the day the sisters rescued Sally.

Blondie sat with her legs crossed at Olivia's feet when she told the story about how they saved a neighborhood cat from certain death. The blonde haired spy was long winded and her story lasted most of the afternoon. The story went something like this...

"A couple years ago, when sis and I were living with the Johnsons, we became heroes because we saved a frightened cat from the basement window of an old abandoned building! The day before we saved the cat we were spying on a group of boys who looked like they were up to no good. That's when we saw the neighborhood bully stuff this adorable little calico cat through an open window. He slammed it shut with her inside! We wanted to save

her right then but it wasn't safe. The awful boy wouldn't leave. He poked around the building with a long pointy stick. He used this stick to flip over rusty old buckets and lift up other junk that was scattered all over the ground around the building. I think he was looking for his next victim to lock up. But it got late… WAY past curfew. We ran home for supper, mac n cheese… and after that we went to our bedroom to decide how we were going to save the cat.

I drew a map of all the doors that led in and out of the building just in case we got in trouble or the mission turned dangerous and we needed to get out really fast. Sis made a list of the things we needed for our mission. A flashlight was the first thing on her list. We messed up and forgot to bring one the last time we went inside the dark warehouse. It was a big mistake and it almost got us killed! At the end of the list little sis wrote the word "SNACKS" in big letters.

I remember that we could hardly sleep that night. Sis tossed and turned and I think I mumbled in my sleep. We were so worried about the little cat locked inside the building without food or water. We decided to call her Sally. This cat was about to earn her second life, so I insisted that she deserved a name like Sally after our next door neighbor. Our neighbor named Sally had survived cancer twice! Sis and I both agreed the name was perfect.

As soon as it was morning we got out of bed, got dressed and packed our lunches way before the usual time when we normally left for school. Then, instead of catching the bus we snuck over to the old building to rescue Sally. When we got to the warehouse on Eighty-Fourth Street we snuck around to the back alley because it was far away from the street, and we knew nobody would see us back there. Besides that, we knew the lock on the door at the back steps was broken. We knew how to get in the building because we had been inside it before.

The last time we went inside was because we were curious and wanted to check out the little tapping sounds on the window and the creaking noise we heard coming from the doors. It sounded like they were opening and closing, over and over again. But, we ended up kinda disappointed because we didn't find any big unsolved mysteries or anything. I'm not sure what we had expected to find… maybe a magical place just like the one in the book "The Lion, the Witch and the Wardrobe" when the wardrobe door led the kids to a really cool world called Narnia. Even a crime scene like the ones in our mystery books would have been better than nothing. At first it was really super boring inside but then it got really super scary!

We slid through a creaky door into this room that was really dark. There were lots of rusty old machines that were falling into pieces ALL over the floor. They kind of looked like broken bones falling off the building. We kept going even though it was pretty dark and eerie and I tripped on hunks of metal a couple times before we found anything interesting. Then, (she smiled) we thought maybe we had found something really cool right in the middle of a bunch of old junk! It was an old contraption with these really awesome giant gears. There was a big handle on one side that was caked in black soot. Sis wanted to pull the handle on the crank… we wondered if the giant gears still moved. She looked back at me before she grabbed the handle. I was cheering her on with a thumbs up. Red used her whole body when she gave it a big tug. You won't believe what happened next! It was so, so scary! A fluttery black blob of winged beasts filled the room!! We covered our ears on account of the horribly loud screeches from a huge cloud of bats dipping and diving around us (squEEEAL!!). They dove at our heads and one of them even pulled my hair, I swear it's true! We've seen a lot of scary movies, so we knew they were searching for blood, OUR blood! We covered our heads with our arms and then it happened, I felt something soft and leathery flapping over my face. I thought I was going to faint dead away, I was covered with hundreds of black monsters with blood-red eyes and bloodthirsty fangs! I grabbed my sister's hand and we ran out the door. We fell to the ground holding our chests because we couldn't breathe. That was the last time we had dared to get anywhere near that building. We even avoided peeking in the windows and we wouldn't dream of going inside… until duty called and we had to risk another gastly attack to save the cat.

So back to Sally's rescue… as we stood in front of the door, I noticed the lock was broken. It was a good thing too because it looked really old like it needed a skeleton key which, of course, we didn't have. Sis and I were super nervous and took a deep breath before we walked inside poor little Sally's prison. I patted my sister's head to comfort her then we joined hands as we walked through the door. But as soon as we were inside we smelled a NASTY odor that made me gage! It stopped us from going any further. I grabbed my chest and choked! I almost threw up too… but luckily I didn't. Then I told Red, "Stop right there Sis" and I pointed "bones, I see bones!"

Her hand squeezed mine and I saw a little tear run down her cheek. We were about to turn and run out the door just as Sally bounced around the corner. I scooped her up and we were gone. I set her on the ground outside and then we looked at eachother. Sis sent me a wink at the very same time the little cat looked back at us. I'm sure she was trying to say "thank you" because we saved her life. We were so happy! We jumped up and down and celebrated our success with a high-five. (Blondie then turned and high-fived her sister).

After we saved the cat which made us feel like heroes for a day, we skipped off to the high meadow. The one we called Moss Hill- my idea. We decided to name our favorite spot after the sphagnum moss that looked like it swallowed the trees. The moss was so long it fell all the way to the ground. We used to play hide and seek underneath it when we were little. Nobody knew about Moss Hill, it was our secret place, it wasn't very far from our house and it was completely out of sight of our school. So nobody ever knew we were there.

We made flower chains and wore them on our heads, like crowns. I declared my sis 'Madame Red, Queen of Moss Kingdom' (Blondie giggled). Sis always curtsied and twirled around with a crown on her head until she felt dizzy and then she tumbled to the ground. We spent most of the morning playing in the huge grasses covering the hill. We rolled and tumbled down the hills until the knees of our pants were covered in grass stains. When we were so tired when we laid on the ground and looked up at the big blobs of fluffy white that floated through the blue sky, looking like it was never ending. We watched the black birds who stretched their wings and drifted above us without making any sounds.

It was an almost perfect day until I told Red about my fears that the parents were up to something. I was pretty sure they had a secret because they had been talking in extra quiet voices behind closed doors. I don't think my sister wanted to hear it. She stopped paying any attention to me and rolled to her side then she curled up like a fawn, listening to the tree frogs who chirped their loud songs from the woods. After that we buried our packed lunches under a tree and shared a box of cheese crackers and a bottle of cola instead of our crappy bologna sandwiches. Lucky us, Sis had secretly taken the cola and crackers from the kitchen when we left that morning. We felt better with lots of energy after a snack and ran through the high meadow chasing butterflies. Then we made dandelion chains until it was time for school to let out. I was pretty clever when I borrowed the mother's watch from her jewelry box and set an alarm for three o'clock. We walked home just like it was any other day, so the parents had no reason to get suspicious.

Sis and I hesitated before we opened the back door to the kitchen. We smelled trouble, when we heard our foster mother using curse words as she hung up the phone. Sis looked over at me and rolled her eyes. I guess Principal Brant called just before we got home. Our foster parents were REALLY mad, furious actually! They wanted to know what was so important to take us out of school, THIS time. This wasn't the first time we missed a day of school because we were spying. We were punished again for skipping school and sent to bed early before we could watch our favorite show "Spy Kids." I whispered to my sister that it was so worth it and I'd do it all over again to save the little cat. Sis nodded and smiled. I'm sure she was remembering the thankful look on Sally's face. Sis was still smiling when she slid under the covers and went to sleep. That's when I laid my head on the pillow and imagined little Sally back home, curled into a half moon at the end of her little girl's bed, fast asleep.

Once Blondie was finished with her story, she stood up quietly and took a moment to stretch and then bowed as a satisfying smile took over her lips. Olivia and her friends spent many afternoons with Little Red braiding her hair and Blondie as the storyteller, who barely took a breath when she talked. Olivia loved the way Blondie talked about the things she and her sister had done. Blondie was sweet but never stopped talking and when she wasn't talking she hummed. All the chatter sometimes made Olivia tired. Blondie usually hummed when she brushed Olivia's hair and often brought an old hair brush from home to use on Olivia's tattered mane. Sometimes she shared secrets with Olivia who especially loved it when Blondie talked about the sister-plan to rescue her from the despicable place that was unjustly called a farm. Blondie held Olivia's face in her hands when she promised that someday they would come with daddy's big truck and drive Olivia to the barn behind their house. She assured Olivia that only kind animals would be allowed to live in the barn and she would always have plenty of hay to eat. Olivia believed every word. She knew her little friends would save her just as they had rescued little Sally from the abandoned building on Eighty-Fourth Street.

Olivia looked forward to the spy sisters visits. It was the best part of her day. She knew it was almost time for the sisters to arrive when she heard the squealing brakes of the school bus as it stopped in front of their house just up the road. Olivia stood ready in anticipation of their darling faces when they appeared over the pasture fence. But every day just before the sisters arrived another familiar figure appeared on the hillside behind the gate. Billy was a young boy who lived next door. He never came close enough for he and Olivia to formally meet but she knew Billy just the same. Olivia knew him on the inside and that's what really counted. Sometimes all the talkin' and doin' got in the way for Olivia. She preferred a silent language that didn't require a lengthy conversation. Billy and Olivia didn't need words they enjoyed the silent connection between them. He too waited for the sound of the school bus as it made it's afternoon stop at the spy sisters' door. Minutes after the squealing of brakes he appeared high upon the hillside overlooking the farm. There he sat silently while he watched the girls tend to her needs. He never approached or said a word just sat very stoic and lifeless. The spy sisters occasionally waved and Blondie called out on more than one occasion but Billy barely blinked and never answered. One day the little blonde spy couldn't resist her curiosity any longer so she walked toward Billy smiling. "Hi there little boy, what's your name? Do you want to join us?" He immediately ran away without making a sound. The next day Blondie told her sister and Olivia that she had asked their foster mother about the neighbor boy. The mother said that his name was Billy, he was special, something about him being Downs. Olivia already knew he was special. She knew it from the first moment their eyes had met over the distant horizon. They connected and communicated, without expression or words. They were in separate worlds; together but apart every afternoon as their eyes locked into a language all their own.

The girls' daily visits lasted for a couple years until something happened. One day stretched into two and then three without the sisters visiting the farm. The girls were suddenly gone and Olivia was worried. The sisters lives, like hers, had been difficult and sometimes dangerous. Being part of the foster care system, tossed around from house to house hadn't been easy for them. The sisters always felt unwanted and like they didn't fit in or measure up to their friends who had "real families." Blondie tried to explain her feeling to the school counselor. She said she felt like a big fish caught on a hook, yanked out of a rapidly flowing stream. She said she had used all of her strength to get away but never quite made it up stream where the water was calmer and life was easy. The new foster parents were so excited about their catch at first but the excitement faded quickly. Once the parents changed their minds the girls were thrown back into the rough waters once again.

Olivia missed her friends and hoped they were safe. She worried something bad may have happened to them. The fate of the disappearing horses was something Olivia didn't want to think about and now the little sisters were missing too. She wondered and worried about her friends. They were all she could think about. The sisters had promised the world to Olivia and now it appeared they were gone. Olivia felt confused because she was sure they wouldn't leave without saying goodbye. She was afraid they were yanked away and placed somewhere against their will but hoped instead that the girls had finally found a permanent home. She never got to say goodbye and waited patiently every day for months to hear the school bus stop at the spy sisters' house. She wished she could hear their giggles rise over the hill once again as they made their way to her. But she never heard their giggles or saw their faces - Olivia never saw her friends ever again. Their promise withered away like her heart and she was left alone without hope and without friends once again. As Olivia stood and waited for her friends to return a tear melted on her hot cheek when it slid down her face.

After a few days, Billy stopped pacing the hill in anticipation of the girls' visit. Instead, he sat in silence and stared all afternoon. The sight of him on the hillside brought Olivia comfort. They were the same, two lonely souls, empty, breathing the same air. She was sad that her friends were gone but the girls were still in her head and in her heart. Their friendship taught Olivia about kindness and gave her hope and a promise. She was sure the girls would some day return to her or instead send a kind friend in their place.

The Spy Sisters

"

I never knew what it felt to be her daughter
even though I chased her shadow through
a lifetime of empty rooms.

"

I thought for sure I would throw up right there on the front lawn… where the neighbors, the men who were carrying furniture out of the house and the parents could see me. I was shocked and couldn't believe my eyes, that afternoon when we came home from school and saw a moving truck in front of our house. I didn't understand what was happening. Why were there strange men packing away our things in a truck with the words "**Big Al's Moving Service**" in giant letters on the side? The parents acted surprised by my tears. They said we were moving to a new home far away. *Why?* I wanted to scream. The parents just stood there with a stupid look on their faces, unable to understand my pain. That for sure was one of the worst days of my life. I knew Blondie felt the same way because she fell to her knees in tears and my big sister never cried. I wanted to scream *no, no, no,* you can't make me leave Olivia. But of course… I couldn't. I felt useless and was sure I wouldn't survive another minute without a voice. I wanted to ask the parents why they never told us we were leaving our home and abandoning poor Olivia. Why didn't they ask Sis and I if we wanted to move before they packed up our whole world and chucked it all in a box? It was as if we were just another piece of their belongings, nothing important and like we didn't really matter at all. I guess they never considered what Sis and I wanted… to be important. I hated them for that. I hated being a child and I especially hated the fact that I was unable to speak.

We moved to West Virginia shortly after being adopted by the Silvers. They had been planning the move for months but they never bothered to tell us. They had to wait until the adoption process was completed before they could take us across state lines. My sister and I were angry that the parents kept the move a secret. It seemed to me like our whole lives had been decided behind closed doors without us. Everything was a secret and nobody ever asked us what we wanted. We never knew what kind of door we would find ourselves in front of or who might be standing behind it. Why was it always someone else who decided what was best for us? Did it simply never occur to grownups that kids might want a say in their lives or an opportunity to choose their foster parents? My sister and I had always referred to our foster parents as "the parents" so we would never, ever get too attached. Even though the parents HAD apparently adopted us, I wasn't yet comfortable enough to think of them as anything remotely permanent and definitely not my mom and dad.

I ran up to my bedroom, sobbing all the way and took to my bed. My tears soaked the mattress and left a giant wet spot where the sheets should have been. My sheets had been removed and stuffed into a box in the corner. Everything in our bedroom was taken apart and thrown in a box like trash. We never felt like anything truly belonged to us. Sometimes I looked at the skin on my arms and put my fingers over my lips to feel my breath. It felt like mine but it really wasn't. It belonged to no one. Blondie was upset too. She stomped her foot and shouted, "did you ever think to ask what we wanted? Of course you didn't because adults never do!" Then, she stormed off to her bed beside me. A few minutes later we heard the mother crying and almost felt bad like maybe we had been too harsh. We knew that we had most likely never given any of our foster parents a chance. Over all the years and in every home we acted out in efforts to take back some control of our lives. Blondie was usually the instigator, she said she was just doing it to protect me from getting too attached but the bad behavior always resulted in the parents rejecting us and then off we would go to yet another trial run with a new set of parents. I didn't blame my sister and she was probably right about how important it was to make the first move. The rejection didn't seem so painful when we made it happen. I had always trusted my sister and went along with whatever she said. She had been making a mess of things for a long time but I knew she had my best interest at heart. At least we were together, me and my sister. I knew I could survive almost anything as long as my sister was by my side.

That's why we finally gave in and decided to go along with the adoption and stay with the Silvers because at the very least we would be together. It wasn't going to be easy but Sis and I had spent our lives bouncing from one family to another, changing schools, making and losing friends over and over again. Friends and parents became replaceable. Starting over was difficult in the beginning but it wasn't long before it was easy and expected. We were warned by our case worker that the older my sister and I got the more difficult it was going to be to keep us together. By going along with the adoption we made a choice to be a family, even if it meant moving away. I was tired of fighting and done with not knowing WHO was on the other side of each new door. I knew that nobody would ever be perfect and even though I wasn't ready to forgive them, the door that stood before us in West Virginia was as good as any.

We spent most of our lives bouncing from one home to another so we were happy to finally be adopted but still devastated about moving away from Olivia. Being adopted was complicated and it brought up a lot of questions and painful memories. My sister protested the idea at first. She told the parents that our mother was coming back for us and we were going to wait for her. So we weren't available to be adopted. But the Silvers told us that our biological mother (that's what they called her) had signed the papers and given up on us for good. At first we didn't want to believe them but they had the papers to prove it. I didn't want to believe my mother gave us away, like our lives meant nothing to her. We weren't anything more than a name on a piece of paper. We weren't important… our flesh and blood wasn't real, Sis and I had been reduced into nothing; something she could just write off and forget about.

I still had clear memories of my mother. When I closed my eyes, I saw her long copper colored locks and beautifully freckled face. The memory of her soft voice warmed my ears and the way her body moved as she walked across the room brought a tear to my eye. I remember that she was easy to like and popular with neighbors who regularly gathered around her. She had many friends and our living room was quite often littered with barefoot bodies, blackened ash trays, half empty bottles of beer and plates covered in crumbs or uneaten pizza crusts. I remember one night being curled under a blanket on the sofa in the glow of a candle burning in a wax covered wine bottle. I listened to distant laughter coming from lips that pinched long fire sticks glowing in the corners of the dark room. As I laid there in the soft light, I thought about how my mother was always so nice to everyone but paid little attention to me and my sister. Most of the time I felt like an annoyance and something that just got in the way of her partying with her friends. We were an expense and a roadblock to a fun life without responsibilities. I knew she felt this way because I heard her tell her friends this on several occasions.

There were few things I remembered about my mother and the memories I did have were sometimes too painful to think about. We rarely gave our biological father a second thought since he had left home when we were so young. Every bit of him, including each article of clothing and his favorite chair had been removed from the apartment after he was gone. Our mother refused to talk about him or even acknowledge that we had once been a family of four, so it felt as if he had never existed. Blondie asked our mother about our father many times and even begged for a picture so she could remember his face. Our mother always walked away in a mad huff like she was offended that we had ever felt like we needed or wanted a father. She said he was worthless and never gave her any money. She told us that he didn't care about us so he didn't deserve any of our attention. Sis swears she had seen letters in the mailbox in my father's scribbled handwriting but our mother snatched them away before she could get a good look. My mother hid them or worse yet, threw them away. That's what made my sister so sure they were meant for us.

I guess my mother must have moved on with her life without us. She was always a free spirit but never a very good mother. It hurt to think that she could just forget about us. I felt like a piece of trash thrown out at the curb. Sometimes I refused to believe she abandoned me and wondered if maybe she was dead and nobody wanted to tell me what happened because they thought I had been through enough and it would just make me sad. It was easier to believe that she died because I had already mourned her as if she were dead. Sometimes I gave my mother the benefit of the doubt. Maybe she had been held against her will and unable to get away or get word to us that she was coming back just as soon as she broke away from her captors. The idea of her being dead or kidnapped was much less painful than the reality that she didn't love us enough to fight for us. There were days when my mother was all I thought about. But most days I didn't think about my mother very much. I wasn't about to waste my time on her… she definitely wasn't thinking about me. Right after she signed our lives away my feelings for her became all twisted and dried up, ready to blow away. Sis promised me we would see our mother again once we had grown up and could make our own decisions. We would get to know her and her friends. Blondie was sure her friends would tell us what a creative soul our mother was, an artist and a hippie who had been sadly misunderstood. I wasn't interested. I didn't want to know anything more about a woman who gave up on her children. But, when I thought about how I abandoned Olivia, I wondered if I had become just like my mother.

Even though I lost my real mother I wasn't looking for a replacement. No matter how hard our new mother cried, I didn't apologize. I couldn't believe she thought we would be excited about moving away from our home, our friends and Olivia. That only proved to my sister and me that our new parents never really knew us at all. Our new father had taken a job with the railroad in West Virginia. We were only eight and ten, when they ripped us from our home in South Carolina and brought us to a new home in a state that we had never heard of. Like always, we adjusted pretty quickly. Sis and I had a lot of practice, we had moved too many times to count. Once we got over the immediate shock of moving, sis and I kept busy getting to know our new place. But every night after we climbed into our side-by-side twins that faced a big window with a view of the starry night sky, we talked about Olivia and how much we missed her.

· · ● ● ● ● · ·

I called my sister Blondie but her real name was Sunny Sky, she called me Little Red but my mom had named me Ruby Moon. Our biological parents were born in the seventies, true hippies who thought it was cool to name their children after earthy things like the sky. The story our mother, Willow, told us was that she and our father had met while hitchhiking across the country and spent their nights sleeping under the stars. The attraction was instant so they decided to give up hitchhiking and instead live in an old beat up station wagon. They traveled town to town working odd jobs until they landed a permanent job at a restaurant in South Carolina. They moved into a small one bedroom apartment before my sister was born. But, my father couldn't keep a job and my mother couldn't stand his mess and hated living in a tiny space with him. She said that's what drove them apart but I'm pretty sure it was much more than that. My mother never liked to talk about my father and always changed the subject when we asked. Sunny was just a toddler and I was a baby when they split so I have no memory of my father at all. We have been told over the years by our social worker Miss Grace, that our mother was immature and not responsible. We were part of the foster care system for two years until our mother walked back into our lives like she had never left. She said she was back on her feet with a steady job and a place to live. The court let us go back to live with our mother until the accident proved her unfit.

I didn't really remember much about the accident, but Blondie said it was all her fault. She claimed to have been teasing me, calling me a chicken because I was afraid to jump off the porch. She wanted to pretend to be skydivers. When I refused, she told me I was no longer her sister. So I jumped. The porch was four steps high and when I landed a sharp piece of metal went through my neck. It punctured my voice box. The damage was permanent, no voice forever. Since my mother had left us alone Blondie ran to get the neighbor for help. The ambulance was called and my mother was in a lot of trouble. Miss Grace said our mother was unfit when she took us away. This time for good. I don't know if my mother knew what really happened or if she blamed my sister for the accident because we never saw her again. I know Blondie felt terrible for causing the loss of our mother and that's why she tried to cover up the truth by concocting far out stories about her. She said we weren't taken away because of the accident. She said Willow had been kidnapped and forced to join a circus that traveled to exotic places where there weren't any phones or means of contact. She said my mother was the girl that performed daring tricks from a swing under the big top. Blondie was sure Willow would get noticed on account of her beauty by a rich and powerful man visiting the circus. That man would come back to the big top looking for her. He would be so taken in by her beauty that he helped our mother escape the evil Ringmaster, returning her to us with magical stories from far away lands. It was a good story but deep down we both knew the truth. In moments of weakness Blondie said she felt like it was all her fault and that's why she has tried so hard to be my voice and protect me from everything.

The Farm

66

*The voice in my head told me to do it. But
then, the voice in my head never thought about
the consequences. Just do it, she said*

99

I knelt down next to Mimi and looked in her mouth, checked her nostrils and her breathing. I couldn't quite figure out where all the nasal discharge was coming from and why. Her temp was normal and her attitude was typical for a twenty-two inch dwarf mare who held her own with her companions who stood a few inches taller than she. Although she didn't appear to be in any immediate distress I felt it was time to call in a vet to do some testing and get to the bottom of her chronic sinusitis. The bills never ended with these little guys. Every time my mini horse's were faced with another health issue I asked my vet if this was normal and she gave the same answer every time; "there is no normal for these little tykes- nothing normal about them." I started out with what you could call normal miniature horses but that all changed the day we met Sully. Something had told my daughter, Danielle and I a year ago, that this five month old miniature horse colt with dwarfism needed us and here he stood next to Mimi biting her neck and egging her on for a game of chase me.

Three of our miniatures suffered from a genetic defeat called dwarfism. It's a man-made problem. Miniature horses are man-made and when you tinker with Mother Nature there are always problems. The effects of dwarfism vary greatly. Some are severely crippled while others are only mildly affected. Sully had crippled legs but a good bite. Mimi had good legs but an off bite and Chip had good legs but a really bad bite that caused his face to develop golf ball sized lumps whenever he was cutting teeth. Needless to say we had spent thousands with X-rays and special equine dentists flown in from Texas.

I've always rooted for the underdog but I was sure my husband and just about everyone else had begun thinking that I had totally lost my mind. Too many times I decided it necessary to save a horse that needed extra medical care or begged my husband to let me rescue a deserving little soul from an abuse or neglect situation. I can't tell you how many times I've been told that money doesn't grow on trees - can't tell you how many times I have ignored it either. This advice began when I was just a child and I'm pretty sure I'll hear those words up 'til my dying breath. I knew it didn't grow on trees. I knew I had a limit... or should have and that the well eventually ran dry. But that never stopped me or at least it hasn't yet.

You've probably wondered about my good sense, common or otherwise and if I ever had any. All I can tell you is... it's there (my good sense) but sometimes when a voice told me that an unfortunate creature needed my help it overroad everything else. This nagging voice was loud and never took no for an answer. That loud voice shouted in my ear...

SAVE OLIVIA!

And I couldn't ignore it.

With my hands on the wheel and my co-pilot in place, I patted Olivia's picture and said, "I got you!"

Olivia

"

Once our eyes met, I belonged to her and she to me.

"

The breeze rustled through the trees with a soft howl and Olivia looked up to the lofty clouds that appeared to be rising like a smoke signal. She wondered how much longer before something happened. She remembered the sisters' promise while her life hovered in a state of limbo. The loneliness wasn't easy but she had nothing else so she waited for as long as it took. Days turned into weeks as the seasons changed. Bad weather and high winds hit the barn. Once the roof was gone, the farmhands took their frustrations out on the herd. Some days were better than others and there were many days Olivia wished to forget. One day in particular happened after the sun had fallen low in the sky, Olivia heard yelling and cursing when the barn door slammed. That was her cue to hide. She knew it was time to make herself invisible because of the monstrous man who played God with no regrets. Once the herd scattered about Olivia caught a glimpse of the wicked look on the evil brother's face, it reeked of desperation and sweat that poisoned the air. His furrowed brows twitched over narrow eyes while he searched the field for an unsuspecting victim. Olivia held her breath while her mind begged for a way to escape his evil hands. Two steps back, her plan was to stay hidden in the shadows until he chose one of them. Guilt bore a hole right through Olivia for such a selfish thought but it was them or her and she knew she wouldn't be able to get away once he wrapped his fat fingers around her neck.

Olivia never wanted harm to come to the other horses but sometimes she felt a little jealous. The inklings of jealousy took hold when she saw their perfect bodies running the way she wished she could. Olivia felt sorry for herself and thought it was unfair that she suffered so much more than they. Olivia held perfectly still as the evil brother's heavy breaths slithered just outside the long moss-hung branches around her. She detected the stench of a daylong drinking binge polluting the air each and every time he exhaled. Olivia felt the night stop - frozen, like a parallel universe as the minutes passed. Her legs quivered, trying to keep her knees from buckling. Olivia reminded herself to take slow easy breaths and not make a sound. The barnyard became uncomfortably quiet while the unknowing was killing her. Fear danced around her while she waited for fate to decide. His footsteps had stopped and she could no longer hear him breathing or smell his breath. No sounds, nothing but her own breathing. Olivia couldn't stand the suspense and wondered what was happening outside her hiding spot. The other horses were absolutely quiet. The waiting and the silence got long and her body grew tired. Olivia began to weave and then lost her balance which caused her to take a step forward. As soon as Olivia took that step she heard the snap, a twig broke beneath her hoof and the snap disturbed the silence.

Olivia's heart stopped and started again, beating out of control. She feared at any moment he would appear inside her safe place. Olivia was afraid to meet his villainous face. She heard footsteps coming her way, getting closer. Olivia had closed her eyes and tried to go someplace else in her head. She didn't want to be there when it happened but there was no way out. The air exploded and the sound pierced her ears when it happened… a desperate whinny, a sad cry, it was over and done, the violent acts of a man without a soul committed against another horse. Olivia was safe. She hung her head while a hot tear rolled down her face. Olivia stood in quiet sadness. She was ashamed that she had wished for it to be another horse… any horse but her. Then her quiet sulk was interrupted by a loud whinny, a nervous neigh and a confident snort.

Olivia lifted her head when she realized, something happened, something different, the herd had come to the rescue. She needed to see what had happened outside her secluded space. Olivia couldn't stand not knowing any longer. She took a few steps forward, poking her head through the long hanging moss. There were horses running, kicking and tossing their heads in celebration while the farm hand slipped away like a ghoul in the night; his evil shadow bumping and burning through the darkness. Olivia silently stepped back under the tree, relieved it was over and everyone was safe. She stayed under the quiet cover until the evening met the darkness of night like a familiar friend. Only then was she confident that the coast was clear.

For the next few weeks Olivia kept her distance from the barn, safe and out of sight. At that time in her life no one was worthy of her trust. She trusted once before when the little spy sisters came into her life but they were easy to love. When she thought of the sisters, a strange peace crept in. There were days when Olivia grew tired of waiting and considered running away to search for her friends. She noticed the back fence had been neglected, worn down by many years of weather. The barbed wire was old, rusted through and laying on the ground. She knew it wouldn't take much to break through the thin strands of wire that remained. Olivia thought about running free but she had nowhere to go. So instead of escaping, she closed her eyes and pretended she was in a quiet stall with fluffy bedding and a mountain of hay with the spy sisters at her side. A warm rush fell over Olivia's back and it conjured up old thoughts of her mother resting her head across Olivia's neck while pulling baby Olivia close to her side.

It had been many years since Olivia's mother left her. She couldn't recall what her mother looked like but she remembered how smart she was. Olivia learned everything she needed to know when she watched her mother work magic with the other horses. Olivia's mother knew how to make friends and stay out of trouble. A soft nudge, a certain look, a stamp of her foot or a little nibble was all it took to get her point across. Olivia followed behind her, watching and savoring her every move. Why, she wondered was it so easy for her mother but so hard for her. Olivia had no friends and no allies because she looked different. Olivia wished for a sister who watched over her like Blondie looked after Little Red. She wished her mother was here beside her. After the farmer sent her mother away, she often wondered if her mother ever thought about her. Olivia was unaware of the truth and never quite sure what had happened to her mother. She assumed that her mother had gone to a new farm where she had forgotten her and given birth to a new foal… busy with the care of a brother or sister that she would never meet.

Many nights when she was especially lonely, Olivia dreamed about her mother and each dream was the same. Her mother stood a few feet away from Olivia shrouded in a misty fog that flowed from the breath that escaped her nostrils. A simple nod of her mother's head and a soft whinny begged Olivia to follow her to a safe place away from the loneliness. But just as Olivia began to move toward her shadow, her mother vanished into thin air. Olivia felt her mother's message and was sure she was trying to rescue her. These dreams were haunting and they made Olivia think hard about being rescued. She closed her eyes and wished and wished and wished.

• • • • • • • • •

Olivia's rescue happened at the very end of August. This day started like any other for Olivia. Her belly growled with complaint of emptiness while she patiently waited for the herd to move along so she could scrounge up a few leftover hay crumbs. A ripple of thunder grumbled in the distance most of that morning. So at first, she didn't notice the rumble of engines and the tangle of sounds that traveled through the air. Olivia hadn't realized anything was out of the ordinary until the earth around her began to vibrate. Dust filled the air as she was swallowed by a herd of hooves, beating the ground around her. Olivia looked up from the root she was nibbling to see twenty-two horses headed straight for her! She wobbled as fast as she could to get out of the way which led her right into the reach of a tall slender girl with kind eyes and a good aim.

This tall girl towered over Olivia's tiny body and she felt her rapid hot breaths upon her while the girl quickly looped a rope around her neck. She attempted to pull Olivia toward the rumble of truck engines just outside the pasture gate. At first Olivia resisted, and even reared on her hind legs, but then she remembered the dream with her mother, luring her to safety and realized that this was her only chance to get help. Olivia quickly gave up the fight and trusted that girl. She felt the warmth of her heart and noticed the kindness in her eyes. Olivia thought about the spy sisters and their promise to rescue her.

It made her want to believe in the kind face that was staring down at her, so she did. Olivia walked away from her painful past and together they began the long journey toward the sound of the engines and Olivia's ticket to a better life.

Cali

"

> *A hero is an ordinary individual who finds the strength to persevere and endure in spite of overwhelming obstacles.* —*Christopher Reeve*

"

My eyelids closed against the sliver of light beneath the door and my breathing became deep and relaxed. I felt something happening to the muscles in my face and body. The twitch began in my left eye then took over my cheek and down to my arms and legs. My chest rose and fell effortlessly with each new breath. My body let go, relaxed and was completely still as I fell down the well of sleep just before the onset of another night of turmoil.

"The dream is dark and damp. I looked around to see something familiar but instead I felt a loneliness that lingered like a cancer while a far away whisper crawled through the empty field. I heard the wind sift through the leaves, creating a chatter that spun a monstrous tale. I can't unknow the lies, the evil, and the secrets that have destroyed this place. They now echoed through my head. I wished I had never been here. I saved the ones I could. But all the lives I've failed turned to dust and haunted my dreams. I can't breath through the coagulated air.. thick like blood. Suddenly black wings disappeared into the darkness from which they came. My nightmare - over! Wake up Cali, wake up! Oh sweet Jesus, it's over."

I can't move, paralyzed with my eyes fixed on the slow churn of the ceiling fan. Finally, I met consciousness. I survived another night. "Ugh," I sighed. My bed was wet with sweat which forced me to roll to dry sheeting. I reached over and grabbed my leather bound diary. Then threw back the covers and shivered a little when I sat. I leaned over and opened the drawer for a pen. My pen moved as slow as an injured snail across the page.

Friday, August 30, 2019

It happened again, the dream. NIGHTMARE! To all those souls I could not save,,, I'm sorry!!! Please, I beg of you, don't make me relive this dream again. I won't last another night!

I was startled by the milky face with dark shadows under glazed eyes, swollen and sleep deprived. I didn't recognize that face staring back at me in the mirror. My arms were stiff and my legs slothful while I struggled to thread my feet through the leg holes of my jeans. Ugh! The zipper was broken. Nothing was working, nothing fit. I think it was an excuse, another procrastination. Sam was ready and anxious when she called my name. "Cali what's takin' so long? We're late already!" "Hey Sam, what ever happened to the old lady who used to own the farm?" I needed to talk about something and Sadie was the first thing that came to mind. Talking kept my head from thinking, worrying too much. "you askin' 'bout old Sadie? I heard she moved in with her daughter, west coast or something. She couldn't stand seeing the farm fall all to hell the way it did. Couldn't get outta town fast enough." I tried to make small talk but it wasn't helping to take my mind off the dream. Why do I keep having the same dream, night after night? I'm afraid it may have something to do with my decision to start the rescue with Sam. Maybe it's a warning. "Hey, Sam tell me if you think I'm going crazy or something. I keep having the same strange dream, night after night. I'm all alone in a field, trapped in a velvety fog. It feels like something bad is gonna happen but I can't run or move. Then it gets dark, black wings come at me and then fly away… it's just plain weird! What do you think?" "I think you need to focus on this rescue. Your mind better be sharp. Stop dreamin' and start thinking 'bout how we're gonna pull this thing off."

I don't remember much about the long ride to Sadie's Farm, five minutes out I pulled on my boots, ready… not ready. I couldn't be certain. But the moment we arrived I was out of the Jeep. My eyes nervously searched the grounds for our backup, the state police were nowhere in sight.

The mountains overlooking the grounds stood like a stern warning that trouble wasn't far behind. I surveyed the farm with an eye out for anything or anyone who might get in our way. My eyes blinked and got stuck on the wooded lot to my left. Mounds of fresh earth made my heart sicken. These woods knew all about death and decay. The soil absorbed the debris and hid the sins of monsters silently and completely. My hands shook while my legs almost gave out. I worried, even dreamed about this day all week and it was now frighteningly clear that it was much worse than I ever could have imagined. And we were left to carry out this task... alone. We had to pull this rescue off and once our Jeep rolled up to the farm there was no way out. My fingers brushed over Lily Ann the name of my angel tatted on my forearm. She had been my twin and the other half to my whole. I needed her right then more than ever before. I cracked my knuckles and dared my legs to move. Sam looked over at me, "where do we start?" I shook my head and opened the pasture gate. As soon as I entered the stark grounds a delicate figure drew me in. Below her long lashes, deep within the abyss, I saw her life flickering, fragile like a candle flame on a short wick. Her body was broken but her eyes begged for her life to be spared. She had nothing left, no more fight, just surrender.

She kept her distance, but all the while she held my gaze as if to say "mercy, please have mercy." I heard almost a whisper, her SOS and it forced a lump in my throat and tears that welled in my eyes. I felt a tug and a burning in my chest like the temptation of a forbidden kiss, you know it's wrong but your heart draws you close and makes it happen. I knew she deserved to live but saving this mare was damned near impossible and almost didn't happen. I moved a little closer, avoiding any sudden movements. The whole scene was pure chaos, horses running, hooves flying and my friends shouting. "Cali we can use your help with this group over here." I heard Sam's request but I couldn't answer. I was too deep and nothing could pull me away until I had this girl safe and loaded on the trailer.

Settling the horse wasn't easy. I had one shot at it. My aim had to be spot on. I knew I could do it. I had seven blue ribbons on my bedroom wall that proved it. But rescuing horses was nothing like riding n' roping. Riding was smooth and natural, once the horse and me struck a rhythm we fell in sync and moved as one. While growing up, my life had been all about horses. I took to the back of a horse easily, like I was born to ride. Roping took a little more practice but grandpa taught me everything he knew and he was an expert. He rode in the local rodeo every year until his body had protested, two knee replacements later and his rodeo days were over. If Grandpa was with me he would have known exactly how to pull off this rescue but then grandpa would never have come to a place like this. He believed everyone should stay to their own business. He once told me, "ain't nobody oughta go stickin' their noses into other people's business, lessen they be perfect."

My grandfather worked hard to build his farm filled with beautiful quarter horses but that wasn't enough for me. I had to do something different, find my own niche, something to call my own. I needed a challenge that was more meaningful and life changing. My grandfather came from a different era when people worked hard to take care of their families and then minded their own business. Rescue was something grandpa didn't understand. I remember when he first brought me into the business. He was so proud, teaching me to rope and clean a stall the right way. I learned how to spot a good quarter horse and where to get buyers for grown out yearlings that didn't fit our breeding program. It was fun. I felt special as my grandfather's right hand but something was missing. I needed to find my own calling, something that made me whole.

There she was right in front of me, it was the perfect opportunity and maybe my only chance. I made sure she hadn't seen it coming. I whispered under my breath "steady girl... and release!" Then shouted, "We're on! Woah, I won't hurt you. Hey guys! I'm gonna need some help with this one!" Despite my ask, there were no free hands. It was all up to me and I had to do it, for her... for me. I was surprised, the capture was the easy part. The rest was long and tedious and tried my patience. The sweat from my brow dripped down my face as we made the slow crawl.

My skin felt taunt against my cheekbones and with a clenched jaw I worked the little mare toward the trailer. One slow step after another, her oddly shaped body swayed back and forth. The ticking of time burned my ears. I worried that It wouldn't be long before we were found out and the owners of the farm sped down the hill ready for a fight. I kept my eyes on the prize and moved straight ahead toward the trailer. It was slow going and I wasn't sure if we were ever going to make it. The air was so close I could hardly breathe, sweaty, sticky with my jeans melting into my thighs. I kept moving even though my new boots worked a blister while the hot sticky fumes from the dark muddy earth climbed my legs.

Off in the distance my friend Sam rounded up three little foals who appeared to be motherless. I saw her stop and put her arms around the neck of a colt that seemed confused. He bumped into the others and appeared as though he was unable to see. As the crippled mare and I grew closer I could see the fur around the colt's eyes singed. His pupils were cloudy and distant. He was blind! My heart bled and a sickness rose from my gut, causing me to vomit a little in my mouth. What monsters could have done such a thing? I thought about the kind of people who abused horses and it made me nervous. It was obvious that this farm had secrets that I was pretty sure I didn't want to know. I started to panic, thinking we would never reach the safety of the truck. My eyes stung from the salty drops that oozed out my pores. A little closer, almost there. *Come on little girl just another step or two.*

Loading her into the trailer sounded like a reasonable plan until I realized her stiff walk and crippled legs weren't gonna make it up the ramp. But it was just as well, she would have been mince meat by the time the trip was over. The herd was tough, brutal even, evidenced by all the battle scars on the lower ranked horses. The black stallion alone could have taken them all out with one swift kick. I had to rethink it and figure out another way to get her out. The hair rose up on the back of my neck and a chill brushed past my arm... something evil. My chest seized and I became unable to draw a breath for a moment. The moment passed and I took a slow labored breath in and out with a gasp.

All at once the air exploded… drilled through my ears and into my brain. It felt like the mud was melting beneath my feet as I tried to run, forgetting the slow horse on the other end of the lead line. I looked back to the hill and there it was, just as I had predicted. A whole army of rabid dogs headed our way- the two men who owned the farm and their friends. Mean as snakes, drove their old blue pickup that looked like it had already been through the front lines of a war. No bumper and just one good headlight, the other hung by a thin cable that flapped against peeling paint with every bump. The men in the back of the pickup had fists that flew while they screamed obscenities. All I thought about was my grandfather's words before I left the farm, "Cali WHAT have you got yourself into? You know they ain't gonna let you just waltz right in there and take those horses. Lord have mercy Cali, you're lookin' for a fight!" Before we arrived all I was worried about was what we were gonna do if we couldn't get the herd rounded up and loaded before dark. Those thoughts became trivial the moment our lives were threatened. For a moment rescuing felt more like stealing and saving horses turned into saving ourselves. Caught red handed with a horse at the end of the rope in my hand, guilty and standing in the line of fire - all I thought about was … *God help us make it out alive!*

I looked over to see my best friend in the Jeep driving toward me, "come on let's go everybody is loaded and ready to go except…" then she looked over at my little friend at the end of the rope. *I'm not going without her Sam, I can't leave her behind.* I may have been foolish, but I couldn't do it. If I had left her there they would have shot her just like they had the others. The only reason she was still alive was to produce a little foal they could sell for profit.

By the time the angry men reached the Jeep, our friends hauling the trailer revved their engines ready to go. Me, my best friend Sam and the little horse were the only ones left to fight the battle. Sam got out of the Jeep all five foot of her and started telling the red faced men to back off. "You lost this fight in court a long time ago and now we're taking them. Ain't nothing you can do to stop it." Her words fell on deaf ears and they weren't backing down. One of them grabbed her thick black hair and gave it a tug. The owners jumped out of the truck and the one carrying a loaded pistol fired a warning shot in the air. I was almost ready to back down… almost. If it hadn't been for the feisty spirit of my dark haired friend. She inspired me to keep fighting. Sam was tough, always the confident one. The rescue had been her idea and she wasn't afraid. I'm not sure I've ever seen fear in her eyes, just a strong will and determination. Her street smarts and will to fight got her through many years of battling her messed up family and then the foster care system. Sam had been chewed up and spit back out several times but she always came up swinging. If it wasn't for her fighting spirit I'm not sure she would ever have survived.

Finally, my own determination to see this through kicked in and I began lifting the little mare into the Jeep. Sam stepped around the men and helped me when one of them grabbed her shirt. She turned quickly and then with the poise of a prizefighter she decked him! I'm not sure what happened after that except we managed to hoist the horse into the Jeep. A few moments later I heard a couple screams from the angry men. Somehow several rocks came flying through the air with perfect trajectory. Two men hit, one grazed. The man with the gun pointed it our way when he shouted, "save yourself. I can't be trusted!" That's all it took for us to jump in the Jeep and peel out of the drive. Just as we sped away I saw a figure that looked like a boy on the hill with a fistful of victory rising in the air. That moment changed me, although I didn't know it yet.

Once we sped away I looked behind and saw the men in the distance surprisingly unscathed. Then, I remembered something my grandfather said "evil doesn't bleed". Miles between our Jeep and the war we left behind, I knew we were safe but my adrenaline popped and fired sparks like the fourth of July. We shouted over the noise of the rough road. Declaring how scared we were and our curiosity about the boy… *who was that boy who saved our necks?* Soon, my body began to ache and in time my head grew cloudy with exhaustion. I needed to relax, breathe a little sigh of relief. The fight was over and we had won but I couldn't calm my thoughts because a different kind of war waged in my head. *How would I help this little horse and what would my grandfather say?* I could feel his disappointment and this led me to an awful dilemma about the future... my future. I wouldn't intentionally disappoint my grandfather but I couldn't see myself walking in his footsteps either.

Often times when my mind wrestled with my future plans I imagined a room with many doors. This room was small more like an entryway of sorts. There were doors, many doors, all different. Some of the doors were old with chippy paint and rusty hinges. Some were shiny and new disguised in bright colors but not one of them had a window or even a peep hole to hint at the secrets hidden within. I felt an urging to choose just one, the right one... but which one? I couldn't decide which door led me to my future self. All the while I felt my grandfather's gaze. He watched me examine every door and scratch my head but hadn't bothered to give his opinion, not one single hint. He wore his poker face; the same one he sported so well on thursday nights - game night at the local tavern. But I didn't need his permission and I could hear my feet walking away from a life that wasn't meant for me. Making decisions was much easier for me when Lily Ann was still alive. We either made them together or at least talked about it. She understood me and that saved me from doing any explaining which I seem to be doing a lot of these days.

After six hours of travels in an open Jeep through highways, mountains and rough roads it was over. It was almost nightfall and we had reached the quartenteen farm. The pasture was just a temporary home for the herd while we sorted things out. The land was unused and a part of my grandfather's farm. It was a little neglected as it had been empty for many years. But Sam and I worked hard repairing fences and we made the house livable again. She and I had moved into the old house right away. It was a far cry from grandpa's tidy home but it was exciting and something to call our own. Maybe no one would notice the crippled mare there and wonder if I had lost my mind bringing something so vulnerable and fragile to an open field without a barn. She needed special care. Far more than I could provide. My plan had been once morning hit I'd make a call to get the horse the help she needed but at that moment I could barely put one foot in front of the other, needed sleep.

Morning brought a leaking of soft light through the cracks of an old shade that blanketed my bedroom window. I should have felt better after a good night's sleep but the foggy head and inability to make complete sentences continued. I'm not sure how much actual sleep I had between the tossing and turning and worry about what to say on the phone when I pleaded for help.

When we first began surveillance on Sadie's Farm I had no idea rescuing the horses would be so difficult. Sam was the one who had done most of the preparations and most of the spying. She made three trips to spy on the farm and gathered plenty of evidence. I thought it was going to be easy and that everything would go according to plan. But I was wrong about both- the easy part and everything following the plan. Sam doesn't seem to be fazed by any of it. The abuse, the suffering, the death of so many horses. I guess that's what happens when you live the way she has, where nothing goes the way it should and nobody can be trusted. I admired her toughness and wished I could be more like her. I'm worried about making a simple phone call asking for help. I guess it's not making the call that bothers me so much. By asking for help I was confirming my grandfather's doubts about me. I was just afraid to admit that he was right and I needed help.

I swallowed my pride and made the call just before I headed out to see how the herd had fared overnight. I told my friend this horse was gonna need a lot of help- *she's bad, really bad and it's quite possible she won't even survive the long trip to Michigan!* I so concerned about Olivia and I didn't think I could handle her dying on my watch. I found her all alone, along the back fence. That was when I snuck her a handful of hay without alerting the pasture bullies. Once I looked deep into those eyes, my chest felt tight and I had to remind myself *"breathe Cali… breathe."* One little look told me- the light had faded. I knew she was weakening. I was afraid she didn't have long. *"Live, come on girl you have to live!"* Every time I saw her after that I told her to live. It fit perfectly with her name, Olivia, Liv for short. I noticed the letters written inside her ear. I had no idea how they got there but the name felt right. Her head was low and her body trembled but the sight of her wobbly gait burrowed into the pit of my stomach. The fear of failure followed me around as I filled the waters and passed out the hay. It made me question myself and I felt as though I didn't know what I was doing. Maybe the ride had been too much, pushed her over the edge. I couldn't let her give up and die like that, not after everything we had gone through. Grandpa had warned me that I didn't know what I was getting myself into. I had reassured him that I did but all of a sudden I wasn't so sure. I remembered how easy it had been doing the chores on grandpa's farm because he had made all of the decisions and took care of the hard stuff.

Once the outdoor chores were done, I made breakfast while I waited for a call back from my friend who wasn't certain she could take on a horse whose life was hanging by a thread. Just before the eggs were perfectly scrambled, Sam tucked her dark hair behind her ears as she ran into the kitchen. "Hey Cali, you better get in here and see this. You're not gonna believe it!" She was right I couldn't believe it. The hurricane had changed its path and it was headed right for us! I ran into the living room and there it was, lit up like a Christmas tree on the raider screen, hurricane Dorian was headed our way!

"Holy Mother of God" what have I done?!"

Olivia

"

> *What do you want? I asked.*
> *To live! She said*

"

Twenty-two horses were rounded up quickly and put into stock trailers ready to haul away. The rescuers moved at a frantic pace, it was loud and totally chaotic as things were happening all at once. In Olivia's state of confusion she didn't see the men with red faces and flying fists in the old pickup coming her way. But once she heard the gunshots, she knew they were in trouble. The sound of gunshots and the sight of dangerous farmhands made Olivia want to hide but she couldn't escape despite her desire to flee because she was being held captive, in plain sight. The girls thought about loading Olivia in the trailer but their attempts would have been futile. She was too weak to climb the ramp and the black stallion savagely kicked, then spun about, his teeth exposed ready for blood when they approached.

Eventually the girls gave up and closed the hatch. Once the herd was loaded, they huddled together in the trailer. Olivia heard heavy hooves and loud whinnies, the horses protested their tight quarters and she was relieved not to be a part of their tangled mess. Shortly after the rescuers closed the trailer door the evil farmhands came breathing down their necks. Men with bright red faces screamed obscenities as they jumped out of the pickup bed, their fists clenched tightly with eyes burning in a fiery rage. Cali pleaded with the men but her friend Sam engaged in a pushing game. Olivia's chest hurt because her heart was beating out of control. She wanted to run fast and far away but that was completely impossible with a body like hers. Sometimes Olivia imagined that she was whole with perfect legs- fast as lightning but sadly, when her imaginings were over she saw herself in the same broken body.

The girls were worried about the reactions from the furious farm owners once they found out about the authorities being notified regarding their abuse and neglect of the horses. Fear intensified as the shouting escalated and then a large rock went came sailing through the air and grazed the ear of the man who fired the gun. Not a moment later, another rock pelted the back of the short squatty man with a shiny head. The men pivoted toward the flying debris to get a view of the person who threw the rocks. This gave the rescuers and Olivia just enough time to make a break for it. The rescuers hoisted Olivia into the Jeep quickly and drove away; rocks and dust filled the air behind them. Olivia looked back to the hill. She never saw who threw the rocks but she knew it was Billy, her Billy, he had her back. Their escape wasn't possible without Billy. He was a good soul, Olivia knew it the day their eyes first met. The rescuers and Olivia were lucky Billy stood up for his friend and lucky to have gotten away. The rescuers moved in to save the horses in the knick of time because horses were disappearing almost every day and Olivia's number was just about up.

There was nothing but the sky above and everything beneath Olivia's feet was in constant motion. She couldn't get her bearings as the world rushed by. Olivia was spared a terrifying ride with the herd but she felt vulnerable riding totally exposed in an open-top Jeep. Cali wrapped her arms around Olivia's neck as they sped away. Although Cali's soft hands held her tight, Olivia feared one sudden bump would send her body flying through the air. Cali leaned in and rested her head on Olivia's neck. Feeling the comfort, Olivia pretended her mother was the one resting her head for a moment which brought Olivia a peaceful calm. Their bodies pressed together in tight quarters, Olivia felt intoxicated by Cali's scent that reminded her of sweet grass, sunlight and earth. Soft hands and earthy aroma aside, Olivia was uncomfortable with the close proximity but she was too afraid to resist. While the tall blonde's arms embraced Olivia's body, the petite girl with round eyes and dark hair drove the Jeep. The girls spoke loudly back and forth as they sped along the noisy road. Olivia tried not to panic but she felt herself spinning out of control, her heart beat outside her chest and fear tightened its grip. No matter how hard Olivia tried, she was still frightened because of her memories that reeked of cruel hands and hard whips.

Olivia's eyes closed as the wind clawed its way through her tattered mane. She tried to stay strong but a little tear formed in the corner of her one blue eye. Olivia's frail body trembled in fear and confusion made her head spin. When Olivia's body swayed with the bumps and curves in the road, she felt like she was floating over the farm looking down on herself. A memory of soft kisses from the red haired sister gently floated into Olivia's imaginings and stayed for a time. Then suddenly she wished to go back to the field where the sisters and she had first met. At that moment, Olivia would have given anything to get out of the Jeep and go back to when the little spy sisters were her friends. Olivia closed her eyes and prayed that when she opened them, she would see the darling little blonde and red haired spy sisters looking back at her. Olivia wondered if perhaps this was part of the plan that Blondie had promised long ago. The thought of a new farm with the little spy sisters there to greet her slowed her breath and she settled down while her body softly melted into the long arms that were wrapped around her neck. Beat by beat the rhythm of their hearts slowed to an easy pace in sync with one another.

The trip went on forever and there were times when Cali's arms shook and she complained and moaned. But, she never let go. The top of the Jeep was left wide open to the humid sky and the oppressive heat from the afternoon sun beat down on their backs. The Jeep doors were flimsy, made of vinyl and attached to the bright yellow bars with heavy snaps. Not the safest way to transport a wild eyed horse but it was their only choice and the best they could have done given the circumstances. Time passed slowly and the two girls fell silent, they desperately wished the trip was over. The Jeep seemed small and vulnerable against the dark mountain range and Olivia felt a shiver crawling up her spine. The winding path made her dizzy while they traveled back roads for six hours. The Jeep trekked through the mountains, past fields of wildflowers and herds of cattle until they reached a little farm in the middle of nowhere. It was damp and the breeze smelled of salty seas and troubles ahead.

When the Jeep finally stopped moving and the ride was over Olivia took a deep breath. She was so relieved when she and the rest of the herd were taken to a grassy patch of farmland. There was plenty to eat but Olivia was too afraid to let her guard down. And when all hell broke loose after fresh hay was spread throughout the pasture, Olivia hobbled away to the back acreage and watched the others eat. She remained tucked away until her belly hurt and she couldn't stand it any longer. With a deep breath she nonchalantly swayed across the pasture and made her way toward the herd. The other horses confused and frightened about the move, acted out. They tossed their heads back and forth while the bullies kicked and bucked each other. Olivia was caught up in all of the chaos and she let her guard down when a black horse came out of nowhere. He chased her to the corner of the fence then an older mare joined in and sank her teeth into Olivia's side. She looked back and saw a patch of fur missing and a trickle of blood dripping to the ground. Being wounded was nothing new to Olivia so she continued on with persistence and managed to get a few bites to eat while she was chased here and there. When Olivia was too tired to try anymore, she perched uncomfortably along the back fence... alone. While she rested, she noticed an adorable little pinto who tried to blend in with the herd. He was mostly white with black patches over his hips and shoulders. His mane was bright white and his thick tail was black with an unexpected strip of white running down the middle. He, like Olivia, had been bullied and chased but he didn't seem to mind. It almost looked as if he was making a game of it.

Once nightfall came, things settled down. The sky looked alive with tiny twinkling lights that seemed a million miles away; just like the spy sisters. Olivia desperately wished to see them again and worried that if her little friends came back to the old farm looking, they wouldn't know where to find her. She looked up and gazed at the new moon that danced ever so brightly across her face. Olivia felt small and exposed without the cover of the old willow tree. She missed the sweet smell of willow branches and the sound of the wind sifting through it's tiny leaves. She was tired and there was an aching emptiness just beneath her ribs. Olivia felt parched, as if her body was hollow and withered, destined to float away with the next flowing breeze. Alone had become her reality and she realized that no one, not even the little spy girls, had sent for her. Their little faces, nowhere in sight.

The dark sky reached down with a hollow mouth and swallowed her whole. Olivia was completely alone. It was a familiar feeling but for some reason, on that night, something was different. The pain felt deeper and more cutting than ever before. In a sad stupor, Olivia peered into the wet moldy ground beneath her feet. Her eyes tired, stared into nothingness and she imagined falling into a puddle where she sunk to the bottom, stuck, trapped in the mud and lost forever. Her hopelessness heard the whispers of the cruel Oleander that begged her to take a poisonous bite. She shuddered and then shook off the deadly temptation. Olivia's heart broke when she realized that this place wasn't at all like the farm the little spy sisters had promised. She missed the days with her spy friends and wanted to go back even if it meant going back to that awful place. Sometimes where you come from seems right even if it's bad. For the first time in Olivia's life she considered giving up. But soon the night took over as Olivia closed her eyes and slipped into a wee sleep.

Once the sun had risen, the birds chirped a nervous song while the horses poked around the field. They nibbled the green spikes beneath their feet. The air was thick and sticky and the sky wore an ominous glow. Olivia was confused by the strange in the air. The clouds were boiling up across the sky in a feverish rush while the wind created a deep bend in the trees. Olivia felt a storm coming but somehow she knew that much more than that was headed her way.

Olivia was looking at the turmoil throughout the sky when she heard a snort from behind. She turned around quickly and noticed that the colorful little black and white pinto stood behind her. At first she didn't think he was real. He hadn't made a sound while creeping through the crunchy twigs in his path. But she immediately noticed his kind eyes, flowing like dark chocolate melting on a hot summer's day. They were deep and mysterious in the center, but gradually lightened to a golden brown that sparkled in the morning sun. He nodded his head in a slow gentle manner as if he were begging her friendship.

Olivia had seen the other horses chase him away from the hay the night before. They threatened a kick, turning their backs and lifting one foot. Only now he walked slowly toward her and didn't stop until his soft white muzzle touched hers. He wiggled his lips which tickled her nose. This comforting feeling brought back a memory and she could see in her mind a dark brown muzzle touching hers. Olivia wasn't sure where the memory had come from. Perhaps it was a recollection of her mother before she was abruptly taken away from the farm and Olivia years before.

When Olivia gazed into his eyes, her heart fluttered just a little. This pinto pony was not part of the original herd. His rescue must have predated their arrival. He appeared to be a loner just like Olivia. This pony appeared kind as he searched for a friend in Olivia and she was glad of it. He followed her around as she rooted the ground for something to eat. He was quiet and stealthy which forced Olivia to peek behind every so often to see if he was still there. His likeability was impossible to ignore and she was smitten immediately. They moved around the fence line together for a time. They swished their tails against the tiny gnats that buzzed their legs as they travelled together. Every so often he walked close enough for his long fluffy mane to brush Olivia's side. She enjoyed his company but kept her distance. She wasn't quite ready to fully trust.

Olivia looked across the pasture and noticed the tall slender girl and her dark haired friend had returned and spread out more hay for the horses to eat. The friends weren't alone. They had been joined by two short brunettes. These two were much smaller with long messy hair, that blew in the persistent wind. Olivia watched them as they leaned against the fence and talked while they moved their hands and pointed her way. They seemed excited and it was certain that Olivia had something to do with it.

After a few minutes, the group turned and walked away. Olivia felt a little disappointed while she watched them make their way to the farmhouse which sat close to the roadside. Directly behind it was a lean-to where hay had been neatly stacked on wooden planks above the mud. The farm was damp and mushy, the trees and sphagnum moss were swelling with moisture that dripped to the mossy ground below. The house sat low like it had sunk part way into the soft earth. It was an old house with parts that no longer fit quite right. It appeared sad and broken like Olivia. The paint was peeling like the hair that was falling off Olivia's body. The roof was sagging like her shoulders. A couple of windows were cracked and the back porch was missing steps. It was a sorry house and Olivia wasn't sure if anyone lived there or why she was taken to a farm without a barn and wide open pastures, absent of trees to hide beneath. She longed for the quiet serenity of becoming invisible beneath the trees. This need was a part of her, like the flesh that covered her crooked bones; the instinct to hide will always be there. The rescue saved Olivia's life but she envisioned a totally different scene than these stark wet grounds without trees. Olivia wasn't sure if her frightening capture and long ride in the Jeep was worth it. She might be better off here but it was going to take a lot more to convince her.

The morning light had brought relief from the darkness and Olivia felt a little hopeful because she had a new friend and the tall blonde was back with hay. The other horses felt it too. They were calm that morning. As soon as the girls exited the pasture, the herd quickly got busy eating the hay. Olivia decided that it was time to try, really try, to give this place a chance. She hoped that her spying friends had found a new place to call home with people they could trust.

The Spy Sisters

66

My sister, my confidant, my partner
in crime and my best friend.

99

N ot long after Sis and I moved to West Virginia, we took up our old habits of spying. We were excited to have new neighbors we knew nothing about and were anxious to spy on them, curious and nosy about everything. Some of the neighbors said we were too nosy. Spying kept us busy but not out of trouble. For some reason trouble always found us or we found it. I'm not sure which way it usually went. Normally it was my sister who caused the trouble, at least that's what the parents thought. Blondie was the one who usually took the blame whenever we skipped school or ended up someplace we weren't supposed to be. I guess it was because she was the oldest or maybe because I couldn't speak they figured I was innocent and Sis came up with the plan. That's how things usually happened until my curiosity went too far. That's when the plan and the trouble was all my fault.

We walked down Mercy Street looking for something to do or a little mischief as old Rex who lived next door called it. It was a bright cloudless day when a few of the neighbors sat on their front porches with sweet tea in hand. Because I couldn't speak, many people assumed that I was deaf too. This was quite an advantage for me that often came in handy. I ran ahead of my sister simply because I liked the way it felt when the wind whipped through my long red hair. My ears were perked and ready for old lady gossip when I passed by Thelma and Betty. I stopped for a moment, pretended to tie my shoe and listened carefully while the old ladies complained about little Veda who lived next door to Betty. Apparently Thelma blamed Veda for stealing an old Mary statue from her bedroom dresser. She said she was sure of it because it turned up at a birthday party wrapped as a gift from Veda to her mother. Veda's mother was furious about the blame being put on her daughter and told Thelma she was most likely just senile and had given it to Veda in one of her "senior moments".

Betty shook her head, pretending to be a good listener but she couldn't wait to have her voice heard and began talking before Thelma was through complaining.

Betty claimed that Veda had been stealing from her too. A ceramic chicken, a red vase and four Christmas placemats. I couldn't believe my ears. *Dear sweet little Veda a thief? No way!* She was such a sweet little girl. Everyone thought so. Even so, I couldn't help but despise her just a little because she had EVERY-THING. The birthday parties, the pretty dresses and a mother who loved and believed in her no matter what. The question of whether Veda was really a thief or not was interesting and for sure a mystery for the spy sisters to solve. I couldn't wait to get back to Sis about my eavesdropping. I couldn't really *tell* Blondie about the juicy gossip I heard but I didn't want to take the time to write it all out on paper. I got sick of writing things down and nobody ever bothered to teach me sign language. Not that I wanted to learn anyway and besides... Blondie and I communicated just fine and she was the only one I really cared about. I let her know that I had overheard something that was going to require some investigation just by pointing and gesturing. Sis was just going to have to trust me about the rest.

We went to bed at the usual time that night but I couldn't sleep. I woke Blondie up out of a sound sleep in the middle of the night to do a little spy work. She followed me without question when I motioned with my pointing finger. I gave her the sign to zip her lips so the parents wouldn't hear. Then we tiptoed down the stairs and out the back door without making a peep. The ladder was in the shed behind the garage so that's where we headed. It was pretty diffi-cult carrying a big ole ladder two blocks down the street. We hurried along so nobody looked out their windows and saw us under the light of the street lamps that were much brighter than I would have liked. I had to set the ladder down and give Blondie the zipped lips a few times. Her nervous jabbering put the spy mission in danger. Once we got to five year old Veda's house, we slipped into the backyard and set up the ladder below her window. I knew it was safe to do a little investigation; window peeping into her bedroom because Veda's family wasn't home. I had overheard Thelma saying that she'd planned to march over there and have a few words about Veda's sticky fingers with that woman (I was guessing she meant Veda's mother), once they were home from their family vacation. Since this mission was my idea, I climbed the ladder and pulled out my flashlight to see inside her room. I looked for evidence but the light reflected off the glass and I couldn't see a darn thing. Blondie wiggled the ladder to tell me to hurry it up so I had to do something or the mission would have been a complete bust. So I did it. I think they call it breaking and entering. The window was unlocked and the screen was loose so I just pushed on the sash a little and it opened right up. Before I even knew what I was doing, my body was inside Veda's room. I think I heard my sister gasp once I was inside. But I decided to make a quick look-see anyway and flashed my light around the room. Then I checked all the most obvious hiding spots, like the closet, her dresser drawers and under the bed. Suddenly, I felt all the excitement and pent up energy drain from my face when I didn't come up with any stolen goods not even a clue... not even a teenie tiny one, zip, a big fat zero, NOTHING!

I had turned around to slip back out the window when I saw it. The most beautiful thing ever. It was a statue of a brown horse with a white strip falling down her nose. It took my breath away and brought back a bag full of achy memories... Olivia! This statue looked just like Olivia! Where did it come from? I wasn't sure but I couldn't leave without it. I had to have it. I knew it was wrong to steal but what was the harm, the statue was most likely already part of a crime anyway. I was pretty sure Veda the thief had borrowed or more accurately stolen it from someone. Sis was shocked when I stepped off the ladder. She looked in my hand that was clutching the statue so tight, it looked as if my life depended on it. "What did you do?!" Sis looked really mad. Of all the bad things we had ever done stealing wasn't one of them. She looked at me and shook her head. I could tell she was about to say put it back just as we saw a flash of light spill over the driveway. Giant surprised eyes and mouths shaped like cheerios, we turned and ran through the backyards all the way to our backdoor and up the steps to our bedroom. We both jumped into bed fully dressed and stayed there for the rest of the night. The next morning I knew I was in trouble, so I hid the evidence in a shoebox at the back of my closet. I can't believe we left such a huge piece of evidence behind. But a big ladder was impossible to carry on a dead run. Her parents found the ladder right after Veda noticed the little horse statue had gone missing. Apparently NOT stolen, it had been a gift from her late grandmother and meant the world to her, according to her mother. I'll spare you all the ugly details but I had to part with the only piece of Olivia I had left. It would have been a lie if I said I felt bad about stealing from Veda. I didn't, even if the horse was a gift from her grandmother. I should have but I couldn't. Veda already had everything and one little horse statue wasn't going to make a bit of difference for her. Like it did for me. After that incident I secretly hated Veda, even though I never let on to it. Not even my sister knew.

After the incident at Veda's house, Sis and I promised to act like normal kids and stop causing trouble. Lying, skipping school and wandering out in the middle of the night. It was hard to be normal because nothing in our lives had ever been normal. We were different from the kids we met at school and different from the kids in our neighborhood. They all grew up with one family in one place. We were never settled in one place, new parents and a new town had happened at a moments notice. But now our lives were moving closer to the permanence of a normal family, at least that's what we were told when the parents uprooted us from South Carolina.

The new house in West Virginia was nestled between two oaks on Mercy Street. A simple white bungalow with three bedrooms and one bath perched on a hillside on the edge of a small town that was really more like a village. The sign that stood on the edge of town read historic village of Bond Falls established in 1885 population: 834. The roads were cut through rock at the base of giant hills. The rails that sat halfway up the mountain, guided the trains around the little town. Echoes of water landing on hard rock filled the air as tiny waterfalls sprouted through crevices in the granite wall.

We quickly became familiar faces around the village especially after I stole Veda's horse. Suddenly we or more correctly, I became the favorite front porch gossip of the neighborhood Bitties. Sis and I ignored their shameful looks and watchful eyes. Instead we continued to be curious about everything and made our way through the neighborhood and downtown every day. We kept busy and stuck together like glue. Blondie took care of me. She was the best big sister. We counted on one another for everything because any adult we had ever lived with didn't really care and always let us down. We lived through some pretty bad foster homes with kids and parents I would like to forget. Especially our foster brother Robert. He reminded me of the bully who trapped Sally the cat. Both boys were big for their age with plain faces, evil smiles, and a heart as black as coal. Only Robert was worse, he was for sure a despicable boy. His eyes were empty and mean How could there be anything but pure evil inside a boy who tortured animals just for fun? Our foster parents at that time were Rebecca and Steve. They of course, thought Robert was perfect; they never punished him. They only made excuses for every cruel thing he did. Blondie did everything she could to get us out of that house. She begged our caseworker, she lied about the parents to the school counselor and then played tricks on the parents to make them want to send us back. We both refused to clean our bedroom and acted out at school but nothing worked until the day of the fire.

We finally got desperate and Sis borrowed a book of spells from a friend at school. Macy was always talking about love spells and how she could persuade any boy at school to pick her to be his girlfriend. Blondie found a spell in Macy's casting book that was guaranteed to banish an unwanted soul - like Robert - he was definitely unwanted. The spell had to be repeated three times before his lock of his hair was burned over a lit candle. I was the quietest and I knew how to sneak around without being heard or seen. So it was obvious that I would be the one. I tip-toed into Robert's bedroom that night and snipped a piece of hair from his shaggy brown mop. I walked barefoot through his room because some of the wood planks creaked. I almost turned around when I stepped into something sticky and gross beside his bed but I completed my mission.

The next day when we were supposed to go to school, we hid behind a dumpster until the bus went by. Once the coast was clear we walked back home to cast the spell. Blondie had studied the book thoroughly and knew exactly what to do. We sat on the floor and held hands with the bottoms of our feet touching. We made a perfect circle around the candle. Sis leaned in with a low pitched voice "I banish you once, I banish you twice. I banish you right out of my life!" I then threw the lock of Roberts hair into the flame. The fire exploded with a loud pop. The hair burned blue then green. It was most likely all the greasy hair gel that Robert wore. The flames got big super fast and then the long white curtains billowed away from the bedroom window to catch the flame. We were horrified and jumped up just as my sister screamed. I opened my mouth really wide and tried to scream but only silent air came out. Blondie grabbed my hand and shouted "Let's get out of here!" We ran down the stairs and out to the front lawn. We both just stood there frozen like ice sculptures. We couldn't move, our eyes were stuck to the fire like glue.

Everyone was out of the house for the day and thanks to Robert we didn't need to worry about pets in the house. We stood silent until we saw smoke shoot out the window and then there were flames everywhere. The glow of the flame paralyzed me for a few minutes. The fire made me remember my mother Willow one night when she stood in the doorway of my bedroom. I saw her at that moment like she was the real thing standing in front of me. I imagined her throwing her head back and closing her eyes as she took a long puff on her cigarette. The light at the end of her fire stick looked just like the orange glow of the flames that were now climbing the window. Blondie grabbed my hand and tugged until I came out of the trance "come on, we gotta call somebody." We ran through the backyard to the street. Sis called 911 and reported the fire from the dollar store. The house was damaged but not a total loss. The fire started in our bedroom but the flames burned through the floor beneath Robert's locked closet where he kept his sling-shot and other torture devises. We told them the fire was an accident but the foster parents had their suspicions and sent us back to social services. They said something about trust issues.

Once again we had to pack what little stuff we had. At least half of our stuff got ruined or stolen over the years by other foster kids and most of what was left was burned or smoke damaged in the fire. We left with our backpacks and a brown paper bag full of clothes, a small duffle bag of shoes, my raggedy old yellow blanket (what was left of it), a couple stuffed animals and a small velvet lined wooden box. Blondie told me she wasn't sure how or when we got the box to begin with, only that it had been with us for as long as she could remember. Her best guess was the trinkets had belonged to our mother. It was the only thing we had to remind us of her, Blondie slept with it under her mattress, always. In the box was a lock of blonde hair tied in a petite ponytail with a bright yellow ribbon, a pair of gold hoop earring, a faded Polaroid of a house neither of us recognized and a class ring with a blue stone stamped with the date of 1999. At the very bottom of the box was an old photo of a strange little girl who sat in a wheelchair with the biggest dimples either of us had ever seen, on the back of the photo in black ink was the name "Olivia"scribbled across one edge. That was it, totally random junk to most but treasures to my sister. We rarely spoke about the box or mentioned anything about our mother Willow. It was just too painful for me and ended with both of us in tears. Even though Sis rarely ever cried. She was much stronger than I. It seemed like she was able to handle most anything. She made me feel safe and like I would survive no matter what, as long as I had my sister.

Once we were packed, it was time to go through the whole process of meeting new parents… again. Seated in the back of our caseworker's car, Blondie turned to me and said "I promise you, we'll always be together." Like always, we held onto hands tightly as we were driven to yet another foster home. I leaned my head on my big sister and closed my eyes. I hated the uncomfortable feeling that came with new parents and unfamiliar territory. Blondie was convinced it was her duty to figure out what the parents were like and what made them tick, she saved us a lot of time and trouble. Sis would peek through closets and drawers, listen in on phone calls and sometimes she even read their mail. She was good at it. It was sorta exciting. That's how we decided to become spies, it gave us the power to figure out a mystery and we felt like we could solve crimes if it was ever necessary.

Rescuing animals that were in danger or abused came about purely by accident. Spying kept our minds away from the painful memories that reminded us we were unwanted, abandoned. Being foster kids meant that sometimes we had to live with some really bad people… like Robert. The spying thing led to rescuing animals that day when the bully that looked an awful lot like Robert locked Sally in the old warehouse on Eighty-Fourth Street. The day we rescued Sally the calico cat made us feel more mature because for once, we were in control and able to call the shots. It was our chance to be heroes when we saved a living, breathing thing, even if we couldn't save ourselves. We didn't have any control over anything in our own lives it seemed. We never made any of our own decisions. We lived in limbo where strangers decided every little thing and chose what they claimed was best for us. Our foster parents after Rebecca and Steve were Dave and Elizabeth Silver. They were the ones who eventually adopted us and became our legal parents. Our new parents Dave and Elizabeth were okay but kinda self-centered and not very involved in anything we did because they weren't around much. But we didn't mind that the parents weren't home very often. We were totally comfortable with a life of two spies, alone against the world.

Elizabeth Silver chose our house in a neighborhood lined with what Mr Silver called "mid-century bungalows" because of the wooden swing that hung at the end of the porch. She said she loved that swing which seemed like a lie to me 'cause she hardly ever sat on it and I never once saw her make it swing. Sis and I spent most of our time alone in the house. The mother had taken a job as a nurse's aide at the local hospital and the father had a new job with the railroad that kept him away from home a lot. But we didn't mind. We were too busy spying on the neighborhood and saving sick and injured animals. I never ever again stole anything from anyone. That time in Veda's bedroom had been a huge mistake. I couldn't explain what came over me. Veda must have realized how special the little horse statue was to me when she saw my face and noticed how sad I looked. I almost cried when I had to give it back. Several weeks after I was forced to return the statue, Veda gave it back to me. She wrapped it up in newspaper with an old satin ribbon that had faded into the lightest shade of red I had ever seen. It was sloppily tied around the middle - obvious to me that Veda had the idea and wrapped the gift all by herself. She yelled down the street and asked me to meet her on the porch. When I got there she was hiding underneath the front porch. She crawled out and handed it off to me with a great big smile plastered on her chocolate covered mouth. She said not to say nothing to no one because I might get in trouble if Gracie May who lived across the street saw that I had the statue and got the idea I had stolen it from her. I shook my head. *"So Veda... I guess the story about it being a gift from your grandmother was just a cover-up."* Veda just shrugged her shoulders and walked away. I quickly pulled on the tattered ribbon and the statue came sliding out. I held the little horse in my hands and ran my finger down the white blaze on the nose of Olivia. I quickly tucked her under my arm out of view of Gracie May's bedroom window and with a giant smile on my face I headed home.

. . . .

One afternoon, Blondie and I were walking along the train tracks in Bond Falls when we heard a haunting sound, sad and almost desperate. The cries were coming from way off in the distance. The voice sounded as if it were pleading us for help so we didn't waste any time. We ran down the tracks that went over a creek bed. We knew for sure that the death scream was coming from the tracks just over a large bridge. As soon as we arrived Sis quickly knelt down to the little creature and talked softly until the tiny rabbit quieted. I moved quickly as I bent down and gently freed her back foot that was trapped under the timbers on the track. At first the bunny limped slowly, but soon her limp became a hop and off she went into the forest. This was just one of our many animal saves. We rescued all kinds of animals. A few times we had saved a turtle stuck inside the tracks but other times it was something bigger like a raccoon or an opossum. When we saved a large animal we had to bring along a large stick or some other kind of tool from home.

Sis and I became super popular one day when we saved a small grey goose that was trapped in the storm drain in front of our school. The heavy rains the night before washed the goose into a culvert that led to the drainpipe. The goose was stuck in a drain that was covered in metal so we needed help to pull off the big heavy top. We had to beg a few kids from our school for help. Most were afraid they would get hurt or in trouble. But we managed to convince a few to help us out. Once the cap was off, it was of course me who went down in the hole to wrap a blanket around the goose. I tied the rope around me and then around his beautiful white feathers. Big Sis and friends pulled the goose and me out of the hole. There were laughs and cheers from all of our friends and the goose waddled away honking in a celebratory chant of his own.

Our most difficult rescue was a magnificent great horned owl. The owl must have tumbled onto the tracks and injured his wing after a passing train nicked him in the side. We were sure this was what happened because there were feathers all over. He must have struggled to get up because his foot became embedded beneath the tracks. He was so beautiful that Sis and I stood for a moment and looked at the owl's intricate markings. The lines looked like the bark of a tree. His eyes were cat-like and the giant tufts on his head were so big and amazing. The owl looked exhausted. I think he had struggled for so long that his right leg got bloody and bent around the train track. Blondie took off her jacket and covered his feathered body. She wrapped the coat around him by tying the sleeves together. The jacket held the owl still while I worked as fast as I could to free his leg. It took several minutes before his leg was clear. Before I had finished I felt the vibrations and heard the rumble of a train coming our way. I looked up at my sister. She looked down at me just as we noticed the shaking under our feet. We then heard the distant murmur of the speeding train. The freight train was quite a ways away but it wasn't long before it screamed down the tracks right at us. Sis knew we were in danger and so she hummed while I worked. She hummed low and soft just like she had the day I fell off the porch. She said she learned it from our mother, Willow. The soothing sound of my sisters steady hum was comforting to me and it helped me work calmly to free the owl's leg. I nudged my sister's arm as soon as the owl was free from the tracks.

His leg was mangled and a few drops of blood trickled between my fingers. Sis carefully picked up the heavy owl and we ran off the tracks. Not two minutes after the owl was freed, a loud freight train sped down the track beside us!

We continued our walk through the field toward the village. We both knew exactly where we were headed. Several minutes into our walk I clapped when I saw it and bent down to pick up a brightly colored rock. It was mostly grey but there were streaks of red and a big purple splotch toward the middle. Blondie gave me a thumbs up and said "That will do" and off we went because the owl had gotten really heavy and Blondie said that her arms were beginning to hurt. The owl squirmed and fought when Sis almost dropped him so she shifted his weight to her side. Blondie hummed real quiet-like while keeping a tight hold on his fragile body. We walked all the way around the bend that circled Thornapple Swamp until we came to a tiny house tucked between two flowering dogwoods. The trees were beautiful and smelled wonderfully sweet because they were in full bloom, but the house was shabby in a shade of dirty white because of years of nobody taking care of it. The paint was peeling, a faded green shutter hung sideways on one single nail, the porch steps were missing and the porch railings were broken. But, my favorite part of the house was the collection of rocks on the ledge in front of the windows. Holga accepted rocks in payment from us or others who didn't have the money to pay for her services. The windows had flakes of paint barely clinging to the wood but we hardly noticed on account of the lovely rocks in all shapes and sizes that filled the space. The window decorations changed each year as the piles grew taller and taller.

I climbed up on the porch and placed my rock on the sill of the window beside the porch swing out in plain sight so Holga would be sure to see it and she would know that we paid. I was nervous so I looked back at my sister for support just before I rang the bell. I could hear rustling footsteps for several minutes but I knew to only ring once. Then I tried to stay patient and waited. When the footsteps stopped, the screen door flung open and a tiny old woman with moon-pale eyes and wispy grey hair that jutted out in every direction from her loosely wrapped bun looked back at me. Her skin was horribly wrinkled to the point that it made her face look like an apple head doll. After a few moments of silence passed, she spoke with a voice that sounded like a raven, low and raspy, she said "what can I do for you girls?" Her husky old voice always took me by surprise, no matter how many times I'd heard it before. I was a little scared until my sister spoke up and told the old woman about the owl with an injured wing and a bloody foot. She started to ramble on about how we had named him Thorn on account of his long claws with one partially missing toe that was now small like a thorn on a rose bush. Holga held up her hands and said "hush child!"... "Bring him around the back porch and let me take a look."

The front of the house looked broken down with its rust spotted wood and flaking paint; almost like it were abandoned but the backyard was bright, colorful and full of life. I opened the picketed gate and we walked over a path of pea stones that led us past beds of pretty wild flowers that ranged in almost every color. The gardens were bright and well kept. When we entered through the back gate, it was like walking through an invisible doorway to another world that didn't really exist, it looked like someplace else entirely. There were several bird baths made out of stones and water splashed over the backs of noisy birds in all sorts of brilliant colors. When we walked past a bubbling pond, surprised frogs leaped to the safety of the water. We heard the birds chatting a tune and the constant rattle of animals in cages behind a tall wooden fence at the back of the property. The wooden fence was partially hidden by tall hollyhock flowers that reached toward the sun. Beyond the fence was an old willow tree with long wispy branches that gave shade and shelter to the animals she kept in her homemade animal hospital.

I felt like I had been in a sort of trance looking at all the beauty that surrounded me. I had almost forgotten why we had come in the first place. Sis nudged me along and said "Red, this owl is getting heavy... stay focused." When we reached the screened in porch we saw Holga standing over a dark cloth that had been carefully laid out on a table in front of her. Holga stood behind the table in a long velvet robe; the color of the pale blue sky. The robe was so big and Holga's body was so tiny that it puddled along the floor. She looked as if she had been swallowed by a large cloud with only her tiny head of silver hair remaining free.

Holga said she was a self-taught healer or witch as the locals liked to call her. She said she could fix almost anything with a heart beat and was known for her healing across three counties. We knew she was the local's best kept secret because her shabby little cottage was busy when visitors shelpt toward her door looking for a cure for themselves or an injured animal. Holga cradled the owl in her arms and looked deep into his body as if she could see right through his feathers and into his soul. The bird remained completely still. There was a calm feeling that floated in the air, even the chattering birds and the clanging sound coming from the caged animals became very quiet. Holga laid the owl out on the dark cloth and immediately went to work on what she called her beautiful patient. She too hummed while she worked on her feathered patient which my sister said always made her wonder… despite the distance if our mother had ever been to see the witch.

The owl remained calm and still throughout Holga's quiet murmurs that could barely be heard on account of her low and heavy voice. He blinked one eye when Holga's tune was over and she gave his head a little pet. I swear the little fellow winked at her with his approval. We stared at the beauty of this amazing owl, drawn in by his mystical eyes that glowed like a slow burning fire.

Owls lived within the darkness which made him appear magical and full of mystery.

It wasn't long before Holga had the wing carefully splinted and the foot expertly wrapped, the procedure was complete. It almost looked like a dance when the bird's head twirled around and Holga spun toward us all at once. "There you go" she said when she put him inside a large metal cage. "He will be good as new in no time." Now off you go girls. Stay out of trouble and off the train tracks." Holga never took her eyes off us as we walked back over the crunchy pebbles and through the lovely garden. We could feel her stare fixed on the back of our heads. It felt as though she had reached into our secret thoughts and read all the words we never said.

Just as we turned to leave the backyard, Holga interrupted our walk "my dear Ruby... I can sense there is something on your mind. What is it child?" I spun around and stared blankly toward Holga. My mouth opened for a moment and then squeezed shut and I turned and started to walk away. When Holga interrupted us again. "Moving doesn't change who you are. It only changes the view outside your window... you must choose to be happy, it's up to YOU." Of course I couldn't have told Holga the truth if I wanted to since I had no voice. And besides, I felt a little creeped out and kinda violated like Holga had opened my brain and without permission took a look inside. As we walked home, we were completely quiet. I realized that Holga was right and I had something more than just the injured owl on my mind.

I felt conflicted about moving on with my life and whether I deserve to be happy or not because I had abandoned Olivia. But I don't think that was what Holga sensed inside my head. I couldn't put my finger on it but I thought it might have something to do with the adoption. Sis and I said YES when the parents asked us if we wanted to be adopted. Not at first because we or more like Sis thought for sure our mother was coming back for us. I always had my doubts. But I wasn't so sure I was ready to give up on her. Saying yes meant the death of my mother. The fact that she wasn't really dead at all made it hurt all the more. The adoption felt like my sister and I were the ones who had aban-doned our mother but really our mother had abandoned us long ago. I had to wonder if my mother had ever really loved us at all. But maybe the thing Holga saw in my brain wasn't about my mother, maybe it was about the move or the little horse we had left behind. Holga and her cottage on Wicklow Street usually made me feel really good but this time I left with a lot on my mind. The fact that Holga could read my thoughts and sense when things weren't right wasn't surprising. But me thinking about what Holga knew made me think about my problems. Maybe that's what she had in mind when she asked me what was bothering me. She, of course, knew I couldn't answer. So there must have been some other reason for her to ask.

Holga was always solving other people's problems. Sis and I knew this because we often spied on her cottage from the apple tree across the road. We watched the locals come and go. Some arrived with a sick animal wrapped in a towel and some had nothing at all. Instead, they left the cottage with a package and usually a smile on their face. It didn't matter what their problem was, Holga knew just how to fix it. Everyone walked really fast to get to Holga's door but then they walked away slowly in a happy mood. Their faces looked less worried when they left. I think they felt that all was right with the world and their troubles were far behind.

Although I was sad when I thought about Olivia, my life was much better than before. I felt better about myself, more confident and I felt like my life mattered when I helped little animals who were scared and hurt. My confidence and the fact that I liked myself more must have shown on my face because all of a sudden the kids at school liked me more too. They used to bully me, call me deaf, dumb and stupid or a mutant. But that all changed as soon as I started believing in myself. Today was one of those days that made me feel good about myself. It had been a successful day. The great owl was okay- another mission complete.

We walked along Butterfield Road hopping over the large potholes filled to the brim from the rain the night before. Blondie looked over at me and said "I think it's a good thing to find the owl and save him. Owls are good luck you know. They bring you wisdom and a good prophecy or something like that. I can't remember exactly how it goes but it's close to what I said."

I looked over at my sister who was still rambling on about owls and other mythical animals. My mind blocked the chatter and wandered off to the little horse farm and our little friend. The sides of my mouth felt heavy and sad as I wondered and worried about her. Then I made a silent promise to myself, the universe and to my special friend. "Someday little horse, someday!"

We took a shortcut through the wooded lot behind old man Pritchard's place then turned the corner past the Fish House to Mercy Street where we walked along the curb until we reached the old sycamore tree. Sis and I always took this short cut to avoid passing by the old Westwind Orphanage. The orphanage closed down over twenty years ago. The Silvers told us that the old Victorian home was built in the late nineteenth century. It had many windows, some of which were broken. The exterior was worn down, chipped and pitted beyond repair. The arch above the second story windows reminded me of a sad mouth with unspeakable secrets to tell. There were curtains still hanging in the windows but they were torn and ragged. Dead insects littered the porch and the large forbidding door was covered in thick and tangled cobwebs. We had heard a lot of terrible things about this place. There were many terrifying tales of children who had become wards of the home that were never seen or heard from again. Blondie said she was sure she could still hear the faint cries from the children who'd lived there every time we passed by. I shuddered at the thought of living in an orphanage throughout all my days of bouncing from home to home.

When we turned into the yard that went to our white bungalow, Sis noticed the path was worn and moss had grown where grass had once been. She said she remembered something from science class. "Hey Red, remember my science teacher Mr. Brooks saying moss grows without roots? Well, our path to this house is all moss. Do you think that means anything like maybe we aren't staying here long. You reckon we'll have to move again?" I shrugged but if I could have spoken I would've told my sister, *Blondie you think too much and you talk too much. Just cause I can't talk doesn't mean you have to do double the talkin'... I'm starving let's find something to eat.*

While my sister blabbed on about nothing I opened the door to our house. I hadn't made it halfway across the kitchen floor when Blondie let the screen door slap. That sound reminded me of the old screen door leading to the backyard of Holga's cottage. It made me think about Holga and her animal sanctuary. Sis and I planned to own a rescue of our own someday where we would treat injured and abused animals both large and small. Our plans had grown bigger and better every year. We dreamed of a place with a big house and a barn and gardens just as beautiful as Holga's backyard sanctuary. Sis and I had decided we would call it Silver Spy Farms simply because our new last name was Silver and we were spies.

Holga

"

It looked as if she walked alone
but she was never alone,
tiny footprints followed in her footsteps

"

S wells of black birds soared overhead each time she tended the flowers. When evening came, the swallows dove in and out of the garden partaking of an evening meal. Holga loved the serenity that evening brought. That's when she made her rounds to see her patients with a cup of tea in hand. She checked each cage twice with a low hum that settled and soothed while her earthy scent danced behind her. The evening events were much like a choreographed dance that she enjoyed so much. Holga had lived alone in a tiny house in the village for many years. The old house had fallen into disrepair with broken shutters and peeling paint but she was happy. The old house and Holga had seen many good years together. Holga always said, *if the bones were still good… she didn't need nothing else.* She decided a long time ago that the beauty of a simple life was just too good to give up. She grew up in this house as an only child and became accustomed to her own company and the freedom only allowed by a life of solitude. This solitude had allowed her to be in her own mind, on her own schedule while making all of her own decisions. Holga ambled about her cottage and her gardens at a leisurely pace that had slowed down over the years. She had always been comfortable in her own skin even if she didn't much care for the affects the aging process had on her body. But yet she worried about all the little animals who needed her and what would happen to her dear little friends if she could no longer heal them.

Holga inherited the healing gift from her mother, Sophia. Her father worked at the local sawmill while her mother stayed at home baking bread and growing herbs for potions. Mother Sophia claimed to have a remedy for every-thing. Some of the locals secretly bought her cures while others called it snake oil. They came in search of a love potion to win over a stubborn man, a cure for a persistent cough or the right combination of herbs to break a fever. She tended her gardens growing and nurturing the herbs and plants that made her potions. Sophia was happiest there among the blossoms, the bees, birds and butterflies. Holga's family had lived a rather secluded life, no friends or visitors unless they came seeking her mother's assistance. Her family kept to themselves as rumors circulated about "Sophia the Witch on Wicklow Street".

Many years after her parents passed, she spied a little cat limping outside the garden gate. Holga walked slowly and spoke softly to the cat. He looked up, giving her permission to pick him up. She cradled him in her arms and hummed. The little cat purred when she went to work on his injured leg. After a few days, the beautiful creature was healed. He circled her legs and rubbed his creamy white fur against her skin then purred with gratitude for Holga's help. That's when she found out that she too had her mother Sophia's gift of healing. Her family legacy continued as word spread quickly throughout the village. Before long, her solitude was often interrupted by a ring of the bell and a desperate face or warm box sitting alone at the door. Goosebumps raised Holga's flesh seconds before they rang the bell. There has always been a knowing inside her. Holga never told anyone about it but it was there just the same. She knew when company had come and also knew why they were there simply by looking into their eyes. She was never sure how to explain it… but she assumed it was a family trait passed on by her mother and her mother's mother and so on. Holga continued her mother's ways in the garden, growing the many rare and beautiful plants Sophia once loved. Holga had multiple bird baths and watering holes for all of God's creatures. She was a part of nature, an earthy soul and she had the dirty fingernails to prove it.

Holga once said, *There's a lot of broken in this world… more than these old hands can fix. Most of the broken pieces are fallen by people who are careless or unkind.* She felt her mother stirring each time she tended an injured soul. Her knowledge was deeply rooted but her hands operate with instinctual precision. Holga remembered as a little girl sitting on a stool beside her mother's operating table watching her work her magic. Sophia's healing hands needed no guidance and no instruction, her long slender fingers always in motion, they were perfect;

getting it right every time. Holga had fallen into her mother's footsteps long ago and spent her remaining days healing those that could not help themselves.

Holga felt that the beautifully broken spy sisters were a part of what was right with the world. She was overcome with joy each time they rang the bell. The sisters had been tossed about, living without roots or a true home most of their lives. But they found their purpose when they began helping animals who needed them and that made Holga smile. When she first met the sisters their hearts were heavy with the loss of a little horse they had left behind in South Carolina. Blondie begged Holga to rescue the little horse, letting her live in her sanctuary until the sisters grew up and had a place of their own. Holga told the blonde sister she couldn't possibly have a horse on her city property. But Blondie's sad face and Red's broken spirit wore her down. What Holga never told the girls is that she checked into bringing the little horse to West Virginia. She thought why not and began preparing a place beneath the old willow tree but it was too late. The farm had been shut down and the little horse was gone. After a few weeks the sister's sadness over missing Olivia became less painful while they rescued many more animals. They became one of Holga's most frequent visitors. The little blonde was a free spirit, strong - willed but gentle as a butterfly. She always tested Holga's patience with her constant chatter. Little Red reminded Holga of her mother Sophia. Her mother had a voice but rarely spoke. Like Red had a quiet way with the animals - it was a gift.

Holga was what you would call an eccentric old woman. An unusual life alone fit her and she felt contented to live with the birds, several cats and an occasional opossum. She knew her place and why she was here. The others talked about her behind her back until they needed a healer. Then they came and pleaded her help with eyes that begged but left her cottage healed with a grateful heart. Holga believed our lives weren't shaped by accident. We all had choices. Each door we chose had a new world behind it that led us to somewhere. Holga had chosen the door that led to her quiet life as a healer and friend to animals. Behind that door she had found her special place where she gave the magic her hands possessed to the ones who needed it most. Holga said. *There will always be givers and takers in this world. The givers are the winners in my eyes because you cannot appreciate the take unless you are willing to give.*

Olivia

"

> *Once upon a time, you were exactly what I needed.*

"

Life was a peculiar thing, just when things were beginning to go right for Olivia somebody else's plans came about and messed it up. Olivia finally felt something good; companionship and mutual affection. For reasons Olivia couldn't see or understand the little pinto liked her, sought her out and chose her to be his friend. Her new friend and she grazed along the back fence while they kept an eye on the piles of fresh hay that had been surrounded by hungry mouths. They walked side by side in sync with each other. It felt so natural to Olivia like they were meant to be together, cut from the same mold. Olivia looked over at him several times because she couldn't quite believe it. This was the first time she had a friend that made her feel safe and protected. He had chosen Olivia, a crippled horse with nothing to give. She couldn't protect him and she certainly couldn't run and play with him. What did he see in her? Olivia didn't know but she was happy he saw something valuable that she must have overlooked. Olivia looked into the eyes of her handsome friend. She saw a reflection looking back at her. It wasn't what she had expected. Olivia thought of herself as weak, incapable and broken. But instead she saw something else staring back at her. Her reflection was warm, sensitive, caring and friendly. A fine companion and loyal friend. Olivia began to look at herself differently. She had always thought of herself as being a nuisance and in the way. The farm owners thought so when they cracked a whip across her legs to make her move faster. The rest of the herd thought so when they chased her away from the food. Only now she was different, special and worth a second look.

It was late morning when the handsome pinto and Olivia worked their way closer to the green bales of hay. They enjoyed a few bites together without interruption. She was so surprised the others had left them alone, no chasing, no biting or swift kicks that moved them along. It made Olivia wonder what the other horses thought about her having a new friend and if perhaps this new friend made them look at her differently than before. Perhaps they saw her as somewhat normal and more like them. Just maybe her having a friend made them think there was something special about her, something worth getting to know her for; a reason to want to be her friend. She liked this feeling of being included, a part of something new. They were a pair, her new friend and she. Olivia had never known what it felt like to work as a team, to be seen as they, instead of just she. When Olivia was just a baby, her mother was the whole team and she, a part of her mother; like an extra rib still totally dependent and unable to stand alone. But now, even without her, Olivia didn't feel so alone.

The morning had flown past, the sun was midway in the sky before Olivia realized it. That's when she noticed her new friend standing with a keen eye that looked off in the distance, his ears twitched and then laid back against his neck. He let out a soft whinny. He watched the others as they ran to the back fence. He then looked over to Olivia with a deep stare that she mistook for admiration. His look had nothing to do with his feelings for her but a warning instead. Something had happened - the air shifted - all of the horses felt it. All, that is, except for Olivia. She was too smitten and preoccupied with her new friend to notice anything but the warm feeling that took up residence in her chest. She was sure his stare was one of affection and didn't heed the warning. But suddenly there was no question about his stare and the attitude of the herd. Something broke through the normal sounds that had surrounded her all morning. The caution flag rose between Olivia's ears when she heard voices and an engine that rumbled outside the pasture gate. This hair-raising warning burned through her ears like a red hot poker.

She stood still for a moment, then turned around to escape the foreboding sound. She noticed the spunky little pinto had run along beside her. Olivia was sure he came to save her with his eyes so wild and stinging. She tried to run but she could only hobble along like an injured animal on the side of the road. Her new friend didn't try to run away. Instead, he stayed right by her side to protect her. But he was captured and pulled away. He whinnied to Olivia with warning to run as fast as she could but his warning was futile since she couldn't run. His effort had been heroically attempted but was nonetheless in vain.

Within seconds there were new hands clasped around Olivia's neck, they were soft hands and with them came soft whispers in her ear. These hands gently guided her outside the pasture. She didn't go willingly at first but gave in hoping that she was being taken to the same place as her pinto friend. But Olivia never saw him again and her heart withered when she was loaded into the cab of a vehicle with one of the short brunettes she had seen that morning, at the wheel. The other brunette came running up to the truck and hopped in the passenger seat. Olivia could still hear her pinto friend's whinnies from a nearby trailer. Once the doors slammed shut and Cali gave a thumbs up, they were off. These girls wasted no time leaving the farm. The persistent call from Olivia's pinto friend had softened and blended with the sounds of air that rushed through the open windows as they drove away. Olivia lowered her head and tried to hide behind the seats that held the short brunettes. She didn't understand what was happening and why at that moment was she taken away after she had just begun to get comfortable with her new friend. Olivia called back to the little pinto but it was no use. They were too far apart and he hadn't answered. She couldn't believe it had happened again. Every time she made a new friend it ended the same way, someone had left and this time that someone was Olivia.

The Farm

66

As moments are fleeting
and memories are fading,
Let's venture the words to
complete our story,
As we embark on a journey
through pages unwritten- let's
write them together.

99

From the moment I picked up the phone and heard my friend Cali ask for my help, I wavered. What made me think I could help a severely crippled horse who was knocking on death's door? I wasn't totally convinced I could do it, but something told me I had to try. So, with a dwindling bank account and no idea of what kind of medical help this horse needed, I made all the necessary plans and tried hard not to worry. I packed lite so I was ready to go before I changed my mind. If you had told me a couple of days earlier that my daughter and I would attempt a thirty-six hour drive during an active hurricane to save a gravely ill horse, I wouldn't have believed you. Once we were on the road, I pushed away my worries and recalled another rescue.

Over a year ago we retrieved Sully, a tiny five month old black colt, who had already been taken to auction. An animal broker in Kentucky had purchased him in a package deal with several other horses. When we arrived at the broker's farm to pick him up, Sully was laying in a dirty goat stall unable to get to his feet. His crooked legs buckled beneath him when he tried to stand. His eye was cloudy and ulcerated. This poor little horse had a nose that dripped like a leaky faucet. When I looked at this scruffy little guy I knew I had some work to do but felt confident in my abilities to help him. We chatted for a moment and learned that this farm saw a lot of unusual animals come and go. Monkeys, camels, zebras and llamas to name a few. We paid the man, then carried the little horse to the truck and headed home. Sully required medical intervention which included a trip back down to Kentucky to visit an equine hospital where he had his feet professionally trimmed and a tiny horse shoe made for his front foot. We hoped the shoe would correct his front leg that bowed in when he walked. The shoe put Sully's leg at the correct angle and allowed his body to build muscle to keep him upright on his foot. We treated his ailments including his damaged eye and he has regained most of his eyesight. His transformation has taken some time but he is now a healthy and very spunky yearling. His leg deformities are permanent but manageable with frequent care from our farrier (horse shoer). His feet are trimmed every three to four weeks to keep them flat. The frequented care prevents his hoof from caving in and his knees from buckling. His rescue and the added responsibilities of a crippled horse seemed right and he eventually fit into our growing farm. The farm has changed tremendously over the past two years and it doesn't resemble what I had envisioned it would be from the start.

My little family farm came about after many years of dreaming that one day I would have a farm of my own. I imagined it to look and feel like my grandparents' farm used to be back before I was born. I had heard stories and I had seen a handful of old photographs but mostly the images and ideas of the old farm lived in my mind. Although the barn I played in as a child was empty, I had imagined the sound of swishing tails and beating hooves making their way across the barn floor. When I closed my eyes, I imagined my father and his siblings enjoying the sweet smell of fresh milk that flowed from metal buckets into the milk house vat. The farm of my childhood was then just a relic of its former self but that never stopped me from spending hours there climbing through the barn's empty loft or sitting under the old apple tree that used to shade the animals who grazed the orchard lane. I pretended to feed the chickens cracked corn from the pockets of grandmother's pink apron and saw myself carrying a shiny metal bucket of milk to the old stone house for safekeeping. As I stood barefoot in the wild overground pastures filled with whispers and wildflowers, I imagined the animals that once provided food for the family. Although my dreams of owning a little farm had finally merged with my here and now, I never envisioned that rescuing needy animals would be part of that journey.

My love for horses began when I was just a child. I have always loved everything about them but I think my love was deepened by an intoxicating musky scent that drew me in with each breath. Their mystical aroma lured me into the world of sleek beauties with flowing manes and genuine eyes that saw through you. I was hooked from the start. These days when I worked in the barn, it wasn't uncommon for a quick whiff to conjure up the past. I had vivid memories of the horsey days of my youth. Each time I visited a stable to go horseback riding I was reminded of the many times I spent with my friend John and his incredible stallion. I barely knew this boy but we bonded through our love of horses. He rode my bus and his house was three stops before mine. He owned the most beautiful white stallion I had ever seen. I was envious when I stared out the window of the school bus and watched John's stallion run up to the pasture gate and stand on his hind legs while he swatted the air with his hoof. His parting waves as we drove away had become a daily ritual. The aroma of cotton candy tickled my nose when ever I saw this talented horse. Dude was a specially trained horse who's beautiful cantor and amazing talent reminded me of a well trained circus pony. Dude performed tricks with the flip of a hand, the long whistle John had perfected or a nod of his head. When they came to my house to ride the trails, Dude would follow John's commands and greet me with a perfect bow.

I barely had time to hang my backpack on the entryway hook, run up the stairs while shedding my school clothes and slip into my Levi jeans and tattered tee shirt before I noticed John and his horse trotting up the drive. I grabbed a cola just before I stuffed my mouth with a handful of cookies and then slipped out the back door on a dead run to the barn.

John loved to show off their many tricks. When he pointed his hand in the shape of a gun and shouted "Pow", the horse fell to his side. When he put up his hand and asked for a handshake, Dude responded by lifting his front leg. I was in awe of this incredibly trained horse. Naturally, I assumed a well trained horse would be easy to ride. I couldn't wait to get my chance. Dude was a tall horse so it took a little help to get me into the saddle. John put his fingers together like a stair step and with his help I leapt onto the horse's back. I felt so tall when I sat in the saddle and I was sure everything was cool until he wouldn't move or follow any of my commands. I was confused and looked to John for help. That's when he got a wily smile on his face. I should have known right then that I was in trouble because John was what my parents had called a bad boy- having spent time in juvenile hall. He clapped his hands and my wild ride began. Dude took off like a shot. He ran as if he were a lightning bolt streaking across the sky. He continued his run through the field and into the woods. I had to duck as we passed under the trees and then he kept going and going until I was sure I was going to die! Just when Dude turned toward the highway and I thought we were never going to stop in time, I heard a sharp whistle from John and Dude stopped. It wasn't a nice casual stop, it was an abrupt, dead stop that sent me out of the saddle flying through the air until I hung on for dear life around the horse's neck. After his sudden stop, Dude lowered his head and I slid to the ground. He then turned around and casually trotted back to John.

That was my first private lesson into the bond between a horse and his owner. I learned that horses were the most perceptive of all domestic animals and that they communicated through body language. John and Dude had a language all their own. When John signaled his horse to go he obeyed and when Dude was asked to stop - he did. I meant nothing to Dude and he knew I had no idea how to communicate or control him. I was furious with John, he set me up with his little charade. But I learned a lesson that day about the bond between horses and humans and thought of Dude and John and my wild ride whenever I wondered what a horse was thinking and how to best communicate my wishes.

Experience has taught me almost everything I need to know in life. When I have listened hard enough to the lessons of my past, I've been able to handle almost anything. I've used my years of experience when convincing an abused animal that I am there to help. But when I first began rescuing almost anything with a heartbeat, it didn't always turn out as I had planned. During my childhood I brought home animals that I was convinced needed saving nearly every week. Sometimes it was a baby bird, tiny rabbit, baby groundhog and even a nest of baby mice. Some of my attempts at rescue were a success while others were an epic failure. The baby mice were the worst case I can remember. I found the nest of eight tiny, naked and blind little mice on the ground and took them home. I was sure they were cold so I placed them on a towel inside the plastic hood that was attached to an old hair dryer. I left the baby mice to warm up while I went to the kitchen and made myself a sandwich. Their time in the hair dryer had been a wee bit too long and when I returned to my bedroom they had been cooked. I remember how bad I felt and stopped bringing home critters for a couple weeks or so. Each time I saw my mother sporting the flowered cap attached to the hair dryer I was reminded of the poor mice with their dark and shriveled bodies that were hot to the touch. My mother never knew about the dead mice in her hair dryer... but I suspect she will now.

Cali

"

And the day came when the risk to remain tight in the bud was more painful than the risk it took to blossom. - Anais Nin

"

I loved riding bareback along the dirt road, even though that day the winds were cutting through me like a sharp knife and my horse spooked several times before we reached my grandpa's house. I thought it was about time he and I sat down for a long talk about the future and why I had made the decision to move ahead with the paperwork that allowed Sam and I to become a licensed rescue. Before this last rescue and before Olivia there were days when I wasn't sure if I was going to make it. I felt abandoned when my mother and sister died and I wasn't entirely sure if I had enough fight left in me to keep going. Most days were tough and some days were nearly impossible for me to get out of bed and pretend like I was ok. I wasn't. But when I saw what Olivia had been through and how this beaten and battered horse with a disability, making every step damned near impossible, was desperate to live, I realized there was something precious there... and that life must be worth fighting for. Saving Olivia had somehow saved me.

I freed my horse Fresno in the paddock. Then I walked up to grandpa's door with enough courage to argue my point if necessary but quickly realized he wasn't home when I noticed his pickup truck was missing from the garage. I was sort of relieved even though I had been wanting to get this conversation over with for a long time. This meant I was going to be miserable and quite possibly go insane while I waited to get the unwelcomed task of explaining myself out of the way. I had to find the words that explained my side without offending my grandfather who meant the world to me. He had always been there for me even when I didn't know I needed him. Somehow he always knew just what I needed. I wanted him to understand why I had to start a new venture of my own. I was unsure of myself and uncomfortable going it alone, without his support. I just knew there was no way I would be comfortable without him completely on board. I sat down on the porch for a minute and looked around the farm. There were so many memories, mostly good... some bad. Like the time Lily and I accidently let a few of grandpa's horses out. One of us left the gate open, she blamed me and I blamed her. We tried to round up the horses ourselves until we drove them deeper into the field. Grandpa was so mad but we had to get him involved. It took all three of us on horseback to get them tucked safely inside the barn. *Lily where are you when I need you most? I would give anything to see your bossy face telling me what to do... I can't believe you're gone, can't believe you're not here. I wish... It doesn't matter what I wish! You and mom are gone and all I have left is...* Grandpa was always my rock. Most of the time he didn't have a lot to say. His love was conveyed in his actions and quiet support. Every time I remembered the past I recalled him standing behind me making sure I was okay.

Sometimes he let me fail but then he was always there to help me pick up the pieces and start again. He didn't say much but he didn't have to. I knew how he felt and I hope he knows how much I care. We aren't big on words or the mushy stuff like feelings but that was the Carmichael way. Grandpa said "generations of Carmichael's got by without excessive conversation so why start now." I felt the same way and I'm not good at feelings or explaining myself. But somehow I've got to make grandpa understand.

Fresno and I took the long way back to the broken down farmhouse I shared with my partner Sam. I needed the time, the rhythm and the open space. Horseback riding always made me confident and cleared my head of unwanted debris. It was my go-to therapy and I counted on Fresno to get me where I needed to go without a lot of nonsense. He normally behaved beautifully which didn't require me to think too much. When I was in the saddle a rhythm caught me quickly, muscles contracting and then relaxed and free. I sat back and felt the wind rush past my cheeks and allowed the pulse of his gait to shake loose any pent up frustrations or unwanted thoughts. When I reached our little sanctuary of rescues, I noticed Sam and grandpa out in the yard kneeling over the little blind colt we had been keeping in the house. It made me smile to see grandpa and Sam getting along. I wasn't always sure how he felt about her. Grandpa was holding the little horse while Sam dressed his eyes with more salve and fresh bandages. It was then that I realized my decision and the task of arguing my case was no longer necessary. It was suddenly obvious that grandpa understood and was completely on board.

I walked up to the trio and put my hand on his shoulder. Grandpa looked at my face with a smile that embodied a true understanding. I squeezed his shoulder and flashed a wink which communicated all that was needed to return our relationship to a place of mutual respect and understanding. I don't know why I had ever doubted him. My grandfather had never let me down. He stood by me when I fell apart after I lost my mother and twin sister in an auto accident. That day took my knees out from under me and I thought I wouldn't ever be right again. I took a bad turn for a while and he gently persuaded me to stay in school when the thought of one more day with the kids in my high school made me sick to my stomach. He was my rock and mentor, of course he understood. I felt a little guilty about ever believing anything different. My fretting the last few days had been completely unnecessary. But still I felt as though I must have done something to convince him. Ever since the last rescue I had felt more confident about the decision to start my own thing. My confidence came from our success but also from the strength of others. I couldn't shake the image of the boy with his fist standing proudly in the air after he had pelted the evil farm owners and helped us escape. His willingness and bravery stayed with me and gave me a necessary boost when I needed it. Maybe my confidence was showing and led grandpa to believe in me.

Sam secured the last bit of bandages, then pushed her phone toward me. The cracked screen of her cell phone revealed a text from a friend asking for our immediate assistance with the rescue of two young fillies. "You up for it, Cali?" I looked down at my grandpa with an unspoken question. He waved his right hand. "I got this! Go save the world, kid!"... And so I did!

The Farm

66

The sky opened up and whispered,
"You will not survive the storm!"
She whinnied back,
"I am the storm!"

99

So, with a half-baked plan and fear of the unknown, we continued south for the beautiful state of Georgia. Reservations were made and bags were packed. I felt confident but still a little nervous, as we left the state of Michigan. Fortunately, with the help of GPS we found our way with only a few wrong turns. I was directionally challenged and despite technology, managed to get lost at least once on every trip. On our trip to Georgia our only detour was short lived… but it was a doozie. My wrong turn took us through a rough neighborhood where we quickly got the impression that the residents didn't look kindly on strangers who didn't belong. The deeper we got, the more nervous I became. I felt uncomfortable from the impenetrable stares we received from several rubberneckers who kept watch from the shade of their porches. The threatening signs and bumper stickers displayed everywhere kept me from pulling up and turning around. The houses that lined Oakland Boulevard were small and tidy with the exception of a few empty houses covered in colorful graffiti. The images stood as a stern warning to those who didn't belong. Guns, knives and skulls made my daughter and I cringe as we passed by. I slowed down and looked for a safe place to turn around just as I noticed a young man with a full beard and bald head covered in tattoos walking toward the truck! He had one hand clenched in a fist and the other behind his back and he picked up his speed when I almost came to a stop. I imagined the lock and load as I stepped on the gas and sped away. We passed multiple signs warning drug dealers to keep out with an icon that eluded to the consequences if they didn't. My daughter looked over at me with a wry grin. *"Remember that labor day weekend we died while driving through a bad neighborhood?"* I laughed nervously as I drove the truck for several more minutes but finally summoned the courage when I turned around in an empty driveway. With sweat dripping and heart pounding, I broke the speed limit as we quickly headed back to the main drag where we immediately found our way again. The sights in the Oakland neighborhood were especially peculiar, like nothing we had ever seen before.

My daughter and I were the second wave of rescuers that came into Olivia's life. The first wave started when my friend Cali and her best friend Sam began surveillance on Sadie's Farm after they were told about the abuse and neglect. These brave girls spent weeks collecting evidence and then reported the abuse to authorities. They had a passion and deep desire to be the change in a world that so often preys on those without a voice. The girls enlisted the help of several friends with trucks and trailers and their daring rescue took place just a few days before we made our trip to Georgia. Cali fought hard to save Olivia and both girls had risked their own lives to save the herd. They were in grave danger during the rescue which made Olivia's escape to safety almost impossible. It was an emotional journey that led the girls through a harrowing experience.

Once we arrived at the quarantine farm it was obvious that the horses rescued from Sadie's Farm were frightened survivors of severe abuse. When Cali spoke about the rescue and the abhorrent conditions of the farm she didn't look at me but instead she stared straight ahead, afraid that the saddened look on my face would cause her to crack. The story stopped and started as her mind drifted through that ugly day. Cali talked as if it had happened to someone else and she was only sharing their story. It was obvious to me that this event in Cali's life had taken its toll and left her with invisible scars. Denial of painful reality is as powerful as reality itself. But despite her emotional story, Cali stayed focused and quickly took charge of the task ahead when she helped us prepare for Olivia's trip to our farm. She filled me in on Olivia's poor health and how Olivia feared when a hand was raised or when any sudden movements were made. Cali told me about her desire to hide from the other horses and about her new pinto friend. Cali went on to explain the naming of Olivia and how she found the letters; O L I V I A written in what looked like a child's handwriting inside her ear. No one knew how it got there but the name was staying. I promised to stay in touch and keep her apprised of Olivia's situation for better or worse.

By the time we walked out of Cali and Sam's little farmhouse and headed to the pasture, the sky looked angry and the winds were relentless. The velvety fog was moving in quickly with a damp layer that blanketed the farm. The dangerous storm that was weaving his threads over the farm made catching Olivia a challenge and threatened to halt our escape. *Of course,* Olivia couldn't have known that this second swift rescue was once again going to save her life and that the ominous sky above was loaded with a powerful force. She along with the rest of the herd appeared to be spooked with an inkling that something in the sky was brewing but they had no clue about the powerful storm behind it. Olivia's rescue had become emergent because a hurricane was barreling down on the East Coast and it had taken a turn north toward the rescuer's farm. The herd had been quarantined at a horse sanctuary that fell right in the path of a category five hurricane. So it was imperative that we get her out and find safety before it hit. The entire herd had to be evacuated within forty-eight hours.

Just before we took on the task of loading Olivia, I hesitated for a moment and considered her new pinto friend as a necessary companion and an asset to her recovery and maybe even survival. I saw the special bond born between them. Her friend followed alongside Olivia with a watchful eye. I could tell that she felt comforted by his support. The adorable little pinto would have joined the farm as emotional support for Olivia if I'd had the space to include him but unfortunately, that wasn't the case. I worried about how the separation would affect her. But to my surprise I think the parting of ways had been more difficult for him than Olivia. He chased behind us and tried to pull her away. It was a sad sight that almost broke my heart.

With the storm bearing down and Olivia loaded we said our quick goodbyes with a tearful hug. Cali backed away slowly and our journey north began. Now that Olivia was secure in my truck, we moved carefully and talked softly in her ear. Even though she seemed to appreciate our kindness, we were strangers just like Cali and Sam. Olivia wasn't ready to let her guard down or trust her new team right away. She resisted our touch and avoided eye contact all the way home. The ride was uncomfortable and lasted far too long for a half starved horse with crippled legs. We were sure Olivia was confused and frightened and the ride must have been painful. Because Olivia's legs and shoulders didn't move freely and she had lost most of her muscle tone and strength. She was unable to lay down in the cramped space of my truck which meant she had to stand the entire ride which lasted over sixteen hours. Her body appeared tired and weak so we used a bale of straw which stabilized her during quick turns and rough stops and starts.

Olivia was dented and bruised from a life that had been unkind but she was fortunate to have so many good people fighting for her recovery. Saving an abused animal was challenging, their pain, their fear and the inability to communicate were difficult roadblocks to maneuver. The look in their eyes tells the story, fear of living on the edge with no voice and no control. It's impossible for anyone to completely avoid all fear. It rears its ugly head and takes over when you least expect it.

Paralyzing fear is an uncommon occurrence for most but when it happens it's devastating affects leaves an indelible memory behind. As we drove north I recognized the look of fear growing in Olivia's eyes and recalled the most frightening day of my life. It happened when I was just a young teen. It was a Friday night and I had been on the phone with friends for hours when I realized that darkness was setting in. I pulled on my boots and headed out to the barn to feed my horse. I gave Frosty some grain, filled her water bucket and put out a section of hay. When I was done, I started back toward the house to see what I could scrounge up for dinner. On Friday nights I made my own dinner because my parents attended euchre club. Three or four steps away from the barn I stopped and pulled down my hood to listen. I thought I had heard someone call my name from a distance. I listened for a moment but heard nothing. So, I walked ahead thinking that I must have been tired and hearing voices that weren't really there. After a couple more steps, a chill crawled up my spine and wrapped a bony finger around my neck. There it was again… a deep voice calling my name, a little closer this time. The voice was familiar but not one I could easily identify. My chest felt tight and I sensed something evil and feared my own demise. I tried to get away but it felt like a dream when I tried to run. My legs wouldn't move, the grass was wet with evening dew and I slipped several times. Then I heard heavy panting breaths reach my ear. The hairs on the back of my neck stood up like the quills on a porcupine. Adrenaline exploded throughout my body with a heartbeat that rattled my chest. I ran like I had never run before. His shadow appeared, casted in the light that hung above the door. The dark figure towered over my body with an arm that reached toward me. I opened my mouth and screamed. Then, desperately clawed the door handle until it opened and I fell inside. I slammed the door and immediately turned the lock before falling into a heap of terror. I never saw the nightmare I was running from and when the police were called they seemed rather sceptical that it had ever happened. The girl I was back then was staring back at me from the past and her face was riddled with fear from a night of unexpected terror.

The next morning I was determined to prove to myself and others that the figure chasing after me that night was real and not a figment of my imagination. When I found his black stocking cap stuck to a bush near the house, I thought it was the proof I needed but the fact that it was just an ordinary cap, didn't solve the case. I tried to brush off my fears and told myself it was just a kid at school meaning no harm. I convinced myself and my family of this until many years later when I discovered the identity of who was stalking me that night. It was a family friend who now sits in prison for committing several murders of young innocent girls. When I thought about my ordeal, my heart went out to Olivia and the other abused horses. I couldn't imagine living in terror every day knowing your enemy but unable to do anything about it.

From the minute I had turned the key and started the engine, I felt a sensation of heat like the blaze of an open flame climb up my body. It settled in my armpits and oozed like hot lava down my sides. When the trip first began in Michigan, I felt ready. Our route was set and the compass pointed south, my adrenaline was pumping and I was ready for the challenge but as the miles drug on I began to get wary and question myself. I have always loved to travel but I am most comfortable in the passenger seat pointing out the window at all the interesting sights along the way. This wasn't that kind of trip. It was the kind of trip that grabbed you by the throat and held on tight, allowing only shallow breaths until your travels are done and the engine has stopped. From the moment we embarked on this journey I felt uneasy about the unknown. I tried to imagine what difficulties might lay ahead. How bad are her injuries? How will this horse react to being confined in a small space with two strangers for sixteen or more hours in a moving truck? Was she in pain and was her crippled condition permanent? It was hard to focus on the trip and my driving while my mind wandered. This wasn't really a trip at all, but a mission and we had a deadline. We had to save a little horse and beat the storm. There were times during the drive when I looked at the obvious concern on my daughter's face and wondered why I had taken on the daunting task of saving Olivia. The idea of saving an abused horse over sixteen hours away was bad enough but this mission was far more complicated and not for the faint of heart. Olivia's body had been keeping a secret. Her oddly shaped body hid her secret well. She was getting ready to deliver a foal at any moment. It was anyone's guess how much time she had but it was obvious by the milk bag beginning to fill that her labor could be days or only hours away. I tried to take a deep breath but couldn't, my fear had wound itself so tightly around my chest that it made me dizzy. I started to wonder if I had lost my mind. I wasn't sure how to explain to anyone who asked, why I was adding another mouth to feed. The only way to make sense of this mission was with the understanding that some of my decisions came from the gut without reason. Sometimes I just knew what path to take, even if it looked like I was headed in the wrong direction.

My reasons for being nervous about the rescue were insignificant compared to what Olivia must have felt when she was confronted with so many new and strange phenomenons on this trip. There were many new sights and sounds when we pulled into a gas station for a fill up. More than one person took notice of Olivia riding inside the cab of the truck. Kids squealed and adults dropped their jaws when they saw Olivia. Many pointed and a few curious voyeurs walked over to inquire about Liv and commented on how cute and unusual it was to see a horse inside a truck. We were used to this kind of attention since we traveled this way to hospitals and schools quite regularly to offer therapy to patients and students. Little horses peeking out the windows of my truck had become expected as I drove through our little town.

During one of our pit stops, a man without any teeth circled the truck twice while he scratched his head. Then he asked, "Is that there... a horse in them - there truck?" I didn't laugh but answered politely. He asked if he could pet her. After a nod from my daughter, he reached through the open window and when he touched her head she jerked back. My daughter Danielle explained that she had come from a severely abusive situation and was afraid. The man looked down at his feet and said he knew how she felt. "I got it bad ever' day. My pa hit me when he got drunk." He stood and stared at Olivia for a few minutes. Then he asked what was wrong with her blue eye. "She blind or somethin' ? That's wild man, wild!" When he walked away shaking his head, we noticed a pistol tucked in the back of his pants. This was only one of our many question and answer sessions we encountered while filling the truck with gas. During several other stops, we encountered groups of people loitering as we would call it back home. I was amazed at how different it was from state to state. In the small towns of the deep south, gas stations appeared to be destinations. We saw people in lawn chairs who were huddled around makeshift tables both inside and outside the stations. During one of our stops for gas I noticed something peculiar about the gas pumps. Every space was occupied but nobody was pumping gas. We even had a difficult time finding a parking space around the building. We counted three large farm tractors, two John Deer mowers and several four wheelers taking up space in the lot. Although it was obvious that there was no gas to be had, we decided to go inside and use the restroom. Inside the station were several men holding coffee cans filled with black tobacco spit. They played cards and watched us pass by. There were signs on the restroom doors stating "toilets out of order" a sign not far away read "no water." No water, no working toilets and no gas but they had plenty of chips and candy for sale. The men stared, nobody spoke and we were uncomfortable. I was taken aback by this but then I realized that gas stations in small towns were one of the few public spaces available for people to gather and socialize.

141

The last half of our trip went a lot smoother than I had anticipated. The anxiety I felt as I drove south on our way to Georgia had begun to fade once Olivia was safely tucked in the truck and we were headed north. A lot of my questions were answered once Olivia was in the truck. I no longer wondered how four girls were going to get a frightened and crippled miniature horse in the truck or how she would tolerate the confinement. Although she was scared and flinched every time we raised our arms, I gained confidence with each mile about traveling the distance with her. That didn't mean I wasn't worried or that I didn't expect difficulties once we got her home. Now, headed back to the farm, new tiny horse in tow, I felt confident that our goal to get Olivia home safely would end successfully. But as the miles piled on and I began to get wary, I started to question myself once again. The task of diagnosing and treating Olivia were daunting to think about. The rescue was stressful and we still had many miles to go, the responsibility of it all felt a bit overwhelming. I know I earned a few grey hairs on this trip.

Although I was stressed, I worried more for Olivia knowing that this journey must have felt all wrong, odd, frightening and out of control. The sight of cars that passed by her window and the eyes of strangers that peered over the seats at her was new and most likely difficult for a horse to comprehend. Even though there were many sights and sounds on this trip that she had never experienced before, Liv handled them all so well. Because of Olivia's crippled legs and fragile condition we were unable to get her in and out of the truck safely. This meant she had to stand, confined to one spot for many hours. I drove quickly and only stopped when necessary. It was important to get Olivia home without delay so she could move her body and keep her circulation going. The need to get her out of the truck along with the urgency of the impending birth, forced my daughter and I to get our meals on the run. The look on the faces of the fast food employees when they spied a horse in the cab of the truck was comical. Olivia startled each time a strange voice shouted into the window when we ordered our meal. She must have been confused by the speaker box that sounded human but had no face.

The storm now behind us, the sun began to shine brightly. I noticed not even a wind. It was clear and luminous. The bright sun made me feel better, more confident, it recharged my batteries and pushed us north for miles and miles. The drive in the daylight was easy. It was the darkness of night that brought on weariness and fatigue. The loneliness of dark and empty roads made me long for something familiar, something safe and warm. The trip with Olivia in the cab of the truck started out in the daylight but ended in pure darkness early the next morning. The last leg of our trip felt like forever. Once we were off the highway I saw multiple house lights- a few people were still up. But it was very late and extremely dark, with only a few moon-faded stars in the sky.

We had rescued a little horse and beaten the storm but I knew our challenges had just begun. Olivia's head hung low and her eyes fell open and closed as she fought sleep. She was extremely tired and weak after the long ride. The farm opened her welcoming arms when I parked the truck next to our big red barn shrouded in darkness. I looked over at my daughter now half asleep and gave a little wink. My daughter was too tired to fully appreciate the gesture but her lips curled up into a half smile as she exited the truck. Danielle and I were thankful to have completed the journey. Olivia was safely delivered to our farm and we had survived the arduous trip.

With the help of my husband, we carefully unloaded Olivia and led her to the barn through the complete silence that swallows the middle of the night. The stillness was shattered when an owl gave a quivering call far off in the distance. We stopped for a moment to listen and then continued on our difficult trek to the barn. Walking to the barn was no easy task since Olivia was weak and crippled and had never walked on a lead rope before. After several attempts and what seemed like hours, she made it into the barn and was quietly put into a cozy stall, lovingly prepared for her by my husband, with soft bedding, clean water and fresh hay.

After a few reassuring words were spoken, the lights were turned out and Olivia was left alone in the dark stall. She was so tired that she hardly ate or drank at all that night. This was the first time she had access to food without a fight or the need to run away but she was too tired, too weak and too scared to eat. This long journey was strange and uncomfortable but somehow Liv held herself together and mustered the strength to survive.

Olivia

"

Maybe all it takes to start over is a willingness to try.

Olivia's body, weak and wobbly began to float as the memories of a long trip flashed through her head. The weight of her eyelids made it difficult as they begged to be closed while the world around her fused into one blurry scene. Olivia's head was still spinning after seeing trees and buildings and what seemed like the whole world pass her by. Strange people peering at her through the truck window and voices coming from a box without a face had confused her. When the truck came to a stop, Olivia was forced to take an eerie walk through the dark night to a strange barn filled with unfamiliar sounds. She was so glad the ride was over but wondered where she was. The darkness hid everything from her sight. Olivia looked around the stall and tried to focus on her surroundings, but it was too dark to see much other than the wooden slats that surrounded her. The empty spaces around her almost convinced Olivia that she was alone but she knew she wasn't. She sensed that there were other horses nearby because of a familiar smell of manure and the clumsy thump of hooves on concrete not far away. When the pacing stopped, she could hear the occasional whispering of wind, creaks and moans that travelled through the barn. Olivia listened to the distant hoot of an owl as the moonlight sparkled through a nearby window, casting strange and unfamiliar shadows across the stall floor. She was sleepy and weak but her mind continued to worry about the next morning.

Olivia wondered if she would have to fight her way through another herd and desperately hoped there would be a safe tree, like her favorite willow tree to hide beneath. Olivia's eyes had seen all that they could take in for one day. Her thoughts swirled around, spinning faster and faster until there was almost nothing left of them. The remaining pieces slowly faded into the darkness that was part of a night that seemed as though it would never end. She was too tired to worry or wonder anymore. Her head grew heavy and her eyelids began to close. Olivia's mind wandered between sleep and consciousness, she thought about Billy and the brave thing he'd done to save her which allowed her rescuers and she to get away from the hellish place that didn't deserve to be called a farm. Once her eyes had closed Olivia remembered the comforting feeling when she stood close to the little pinto with his warm chocolate eyes that melted into hers. She felt a tickle when she thought about his soft muzzle like white velvet brushing her lips. A warm sensation settled into Olivia's tired body while her sadness began to evaporate into the cool air. A bubble of lonely thoughts floated overhead for a few minutes before they disappeared with a pop. Quickly, she realized the popping sound was her head dropping to the floor. Olivia's body had grown heavy which forced her legs to buckle. She let out a long breath and nestled into the fluffy pine shavings. A warm tingle crawled up her legs, over her hips and along her spine. This sensation found a home in her chest, rising and falling with breath- she wasn't alone.

Olivia felt them near and saw their faces smiling sweetly in her mind. The little spy sisters were there in spirit, they had been with her all along. Olivia had felt their presence when she first met the tall blonde and her short brunette friend. Their kind demeanor and brave determination reminded Olivia of her first friends. She also spied the wink sported by the short brunette to her daughter when they arrived that evening. It was familiar, just like the wink the red headed spy gave her sister the first time Olivia let them run their hands over her body and through her mane. Olivia started to allow a comforting thought to creep into her head- maybe she'd found a loving home. Olivia hoped the little spy sisters had found a happy home too. They were a part of her, they lived in her head and in her heart. The spy sisters and she were kindred spirits who understood each other. The sisters gave Olivia love when no one else could. Suddenly, she understood as she looked back at herself… happiness, her happiness, was now up to her. Olivia didn't understand why or how she felt so different this time around - this rescue. She just knew.

Olivia began to breathe deeply. Her head filled with memories and her ears were lulled by animals breathing as she drifted in and out of slumber. She erased the fear. She erased the pain. She erased her past so she could accept a new life. Olivia's mind now free, she slept hard and deep for many hours, in a safe place, where the slumber gods gently *w o v e* her back together.

The Farm

"

When you forgive you love and love
has a way of making you whole.

"

Olivia's rescue was a spur of the moment decision. We drove for sixteen hours toward a powerful storm to rescue Olivia. The trip home was a rush north out of the reach of hurricane Dorian to the safety of our farm. My daughter and I are always on the lookout for people or animals that need fixing. When we learned that Liv needed our help, we were ready and on the road at a moment's notice. It wasn't an easy trip but definitely worth it.

We will never know all that Olivia has been through. My heart broke every time I touched her side and felt each rib protruding the skin of her emaciated body. When I sat down to write her story, I thought about all the devastating things that may have been a part of her reality. Her body wore the scars of a severely abused horse and yet I felt as though Olivia had known kindness from someone who cared and looked after her at some point in her life. Olivia quickly changed her attitude from an utterly frightened animal to a trusting horse in a matter of days. This was unusual for an animal from an abused and neglected situation. Her speedy transformation gave me pause and I thought about how she broke so easily. A relationship with someone kind and caring was the perfect explanation for Olivia's ability to recognize kindness and trust people willing to help. She came to the farm in poor health with deep psychological scars. But in time and with great patience she began to heal and learned to trust.

I wish I could tell you that everything was better once Olivia was home and the next phase of her life was easy. But I can't... that's not what happened. The next step was quite challenging and difficult for Olivia. Her health was in jeopardy before she arrived but the stress of her rescue and long journeys had taken their toll on her weak and starved body. She required immediate medical attention for an infection and she needed intense nutritional help for her malnourished condition. The vet did a careful evaluation and took X-rays to uncover the reason for her mis-shapen body. We discovered her crippled legs stemmed from a deformity that forced her body to fuse together over time, making it difficult for her to walk. The test results confirmed that Olivia's disability was permanent. Permanent can be a beautiful word meaning stability. But in this case, permanent meant there wasn't anything anyone could do to improve Olivia's mobility. This diagnosis changed our goals and plans for her. Now that her abused and neglected body was healing, she had begun to live a comfortable life within her limitations. We know that physical and mental recovery takes time but the journey has been especially difficult for this innocent soul.

Olivia spent many years suffering abuse and neglect that brought her within inches of her life. She was rescued just in time. Olivia had run out of time because her health was failing and the extra toll of carrying a baby was too much to handle. We knew that delivering a foal wouldn't be easy for Olivia in her weakened state.

When I got Cali's call asking for help I knew by her voice that her heart ached for this poor little horse, an ache made of equal parts, anger and sadness, her tone was desperate and pleading. My friend knew that the birth of Olivia's baby was imminent and that a pasture without a barn in the middle of a storm was no place to give birth. She and Sam could see that Olivia had a lot of life left in her eyes and knew by rescuing her they were quite possibly saving two lives. So the girls fought hard for Olivia, even risking their own lives to save hers.

One of the reasons Olivia survived is the fact that she was carrying a foal. Her life was spared not once but three times because of her pregnancy. Olivia held out giving birth just long enough to make it onto our farm. Her life was spared by the abusive farm owners because of greed. They allowed her to live so they could sell her baby who would quite likely be a small horse with dwarfism and fetch an inflated price. Cali put in an extra effort to save Liv knowing she was pregnant. The pregnancy played a role in my decision to bring her onto the farm. The fact that this horse was in need inspired me. But the thought of saving two lives was enough to make me drive thirty-six hours round trip headed straight for a hurricane to save mom and baby. I was ready to provide the extra care that she needed to get her strong and healthy and devote sufficient time to watch over the birth and her newborn baby. The day that Olivia arrived on this farm was just the beginning. We had a lot of work ahead of us. It was going to take time to get her well but I had a plan to quickly help her gain the strength required to deliver her baby.

I expected this story to have the perfect ending once Olivia's secret was revealed and she was standing proudly alongside her newly born foal... healthy, happy and safe. This beautiful scene is what I envisioned all the while I drove as fast as I could to get her home safely. But, that was not meant to be. The day I found Olivia lying on the floor of the barn rocking back-and-forth was the day she gave birth to a premature baby horse with obvious signs of dwarfism. I believed that Olivia held out until she had found a soft landing before allowing herself to become vulnerable. After the death of Olivia's foal, my heart ached and I felt a sense of overwhelming guilt. I thought I'd failed Olivia AND her baby somehow. Some have said there was no way for this little guy to survive because he was too early and Olivia's weak and starved body was unable to provide him with the nourishment he needed before birth. But I couldn't shake the guilt and I wondered what I could have done to prevent his death.

The day Olivia lost her foal was a very sad day on the farm. I felt the cold air of autumn take over the gaping hole in my chest. This sadness filled my body and threatened to eat me whole. It's okay to shed a tear or two over the death of her baby. We have shed many salty tears over the loss. But, it's also okay to be hopeful for the future because Olivia's life is so much better today than it was before. She will never live the life of a "normal horse", her disability is permanent but we will do our best to help her live her best life.

Despite the sad chain of events, Olivia's life improved. She learned to trust us and she was the first horse to call to me when I stepped foot in the barn or arrived at the pasture gate. She enjoyed the comfort of a full belly and unconditional love. Liv's curiosity provoked her to follow me around the barn. She watched while the eggs were removed from my apron and placed in the basket. She waited patiently each day to be led to pasture where she received a treat as a reward for her efforts. Liv was happy, gained weight and grew stronger. Her wounds healed and she made friends with the other horses.

Walking continues to be difficult for Olivia but living without threat allows her the time needed to get where she wants to go. Liv has been accepted into a small group of rescued horses with similar issues. She is no longer lonely and enjoys the company of her little friends. They have become a family and look out for one another. Her buddy, a little coco brown horse named Sully suffers from a form of dwarfism. Despite his mildly crippled legs, he's a spunky little guy with attitude. Sully accepted Olivia right away and they have been buddies ever since. Living in the stall next door is Mimi, an extremely tiny dwarf mare with a bad underbite and a personality as big and tough as Texas. Olivia's friend Chip, the ringleader of little land has pinto markings and an adorable face that no one could resist. I have enjoyed watching this little group walk single file through the great white pines to the upper pasture where they enjoyed bites of hay, chasing chickens and laying in the sun. Olivia was never far behind her friends. She has fit right into our little farm and no longer worries about hiding or getting enough to eat.

Olivia has many caretakers which included little girls who brought her treats. They brushed her mane and braided her tail. During story hour the girls sat in little chairs and read her stories from their favorite books. Monarch butterflies danced carelessly across the skies. Olivia's new home was a big barn with kind animals, chickens, goats and horses. Her life with a full belly and kind people who loved her was so much better than how it began. I am so thankful that promises were kept and a charmed life delivered.

Olivia

"

> *What lies behind us and what lies before*
> *us are tiny matters compared to what lies*
> *within us. -Ralph Waldo Emerson*

"

Olivia had shown great strength through all of the changes she was presented with. Constant fear, memories of abuse, the effects of starvation, feelings of loneliness and the loss of her foal were just some of the obstacles Olivia faced during her recovery. She struggled at first to recover mentally and physically but over a short period of time her internal and external scars were almost healed. She sensed the confidence and peaceful calm of the other animals on the farm. They felt no fear, no desperation and never an empty belly. Their positive attitudes gave Olivia the courage she needed to trust the new faces; vets, equine dentists, farriers and visitors that constantly showed up on the farm.

In the daylight birds trilled while they jumped from branch to branch. The roosters strutted and the hens chased each other. The horses grazed and occasionally ran for no reason at all. The goats head butted each other and butted anything else that got in their way. The woods were filled with curious deer who often watched the barnyard animals. The bees flit and floated to each and every bud while the butterflies drifted aimlessly overhead. Olivia's days were filled with sights and sounds but her nights were peaceful and renewing.

As Olivia stood in the field beneath the autumn moon, swollen and golden, she looked up at the giant barred owl that rested in a sheltering oak tree along the edge of the woods and remembered his call the night she was led to an unfamiliar barn with unusual sounds. Her head was swimming in uncertainty that night and her heart beat rapidly when she was left alone in her stall. One of her greatest fears besides humans had been angst of the dark. Many bad things had happened in the past within the shadows of night. But those nights seemed far away and her uncertainty had slowly melted into a distant memory. This allowed ample space for a confident little horse who had almost forgotten about the cruelness of people with no compassion, no heart and no soul.

Her new home was much different than the farm she had left behind. People were kind and the animals were calm and secure. She never went to bed hungry and always had a layer of soft bedding in her stall. The darkness no longer frightened Olivia and she took great comfort in the sounds of animals breathing throughout the night. Their slow easy breaths reminded her that she wasn't alone and in a safe place.

Olivia had suffered from abusive owners and a lot of let downs but she willfully accepted her past when she welcomed a promising future. Some days she had almost forgotten that she was any different than any other horse. The other horses didn't seem to notice her unusual gate and treated her the same as they did any other. Olivia's crippled legs and odd sway were no longer a risk to her survival but an endearing quality of her tenacity and willful spirit. On the days that seemed the hardest Olivia moved forward by an inch and some days a mile. She continued to try and continued to heal, forward momentum was the key. As the days melted away so did a lifetime of painful memories and unforgiving scars.

The Spy Sisters

"

> *You smiled at my face, like*
> *you knew all of my secrets.*

"

I looked around to be sure that I was completely alone before I closed my bedroom door. My fingers brushed over the raised flower design and the earthy smell of old leather tickled my nose as I opened my new diary. A gift from Holga for my eleventh birthday. I could tell the leather cover was old but the pages were clean, no writing. It didn't look used.

Saturday January 4th

Happy New Year

The velvety fog had finally lifted when Sis and I left Holga's house for the second time this week. We've become quite a team rescuing animals on a regular basis. We got a letter from Willow - our birth mom, the other day. She said she gave us up because she loved us too much to keep us. She went on about not having enough money to give us what we needed, a nice house, nice things and so on. Sis totally bought mom's story but I had my doubts. Even though Sis was older than I the last time we lived with Willow I felt like I knew her better. Like I could see her for who she really was; an immature, selfish woman who never should have had children in the first place, the second place and every other place after that. I never mentioned any of this to Sis 'cause I didn't want to hurt her. I felt like I had moved on and done better than my sister. I think it's because I've accepted my life, the incompetence of my mother and the reality of my adoption. I don't blame myself for being taken away from our mother like my sister does. I don't blame Sis either. It's all Willow's fault.

I have finally started to learn sign language. My new friend Carrie taught me all the words that she knew because of her brother Ryan, who's deaf. I liked learning and even started teaching a few words to my sister. The parents said I could sign up for a class so I could learn the whole alphabet.

I still miss Olivia. It would help if I knew if she was ok. Sis and I don't talk about her as much as we used to but I think about her all the time.

The Silvers are ok as parents but I don't think I'll ever feel close to them. I don't know why but I just don't feel it. I hope they never read this diary!

I tucked it under my mattress. I plan to fill this diary full of things I don't want anyone to know. I haven't told even one person about my writing. It was just for me. A secret not even my sister knew.

The Farm

"

Knowing where your scars come from
doesn't make them disappear.

"

The geese gathered on the pond and monarchs in large groups floated on the cusp signaling that fall had arrived. It was mid-afternoon when I finished my chores inside the barn and entered the barnyard. It was peaceful and quiet. As I looked around I saw chickens scratching for worms in the newly turned earth while the goats laid in the warm sun. The horses were busy as they chewed the last bites of hay. But something was missing. Normally when I entered the barnyard Olivia immediately called to me in her husky voice but not today. Her voice and her body were nowhere to be found. Of course, I panicked and ran frantically to all corners of the yard, NOTHING! Each and every animal within the barnyard looked unconcerned, poker faces- everyone. I called out to Olivia but my ask was unanswered. I looked down the dirt drive leading from the barn to the country road that passed by the farm. I panicked a little... okay a lot! While a giant lump formed in my gut.

I argued with myself; *No way could she have made it very far in her condition... normally she doesn't go more than a few steps past the barn. But, she was missing. Was somebody here? Nobody would have stolen a crippled horse, NOBODY. I began to sweat. Had I left her in the barn?* "No, no... *I distinctly remember leading her through the gate with Aunt Vicky's cookies. She was there a few minutes ago I'm sure of it!*

Even though I thought it ridiculous, something told me to walk down the winding drive. I walked passed the white pines, thorney raspberry bushes and beneath the towering oaks. I could see the long stretch of drive ahead that led to a public road with cars passing by. My heart raced and I began to move faster. Just then I heard a soft grumble, low, gravelly and familiar. I looked to the right as my heart skipped a beat. There beneath an old willow tree was Olivia. She sniffed the leaves and admired the long wispy branches with a reminiscent look in her eyes. Her head rose with a nod and she slowly joined me on the drive. Her travel down memory lane complete, she was ready as we headed back to the barn.

I felt great relief as we walked back to the barnyard but still I wondered, *how had she managed to go so far in such a short time?* Walking is slow and tedious for Olivia and it normally takes a lot of time for her to get from here to there. Some things have remained a mystery… I looked over at Olivia and noticed something as I watched her walk alongside me. She still sported a patch of skin thick with scars that struggled to grow hair - a remnant of an almost forgotten past. The life this poor horse has weathered, the cruel abuse, her losses and her harrowing rescues- Olivia continues to amaze me everyday. I have now taken a deep breath and relax in the knowledge that Olivia is a survivor. I decided it true the day she disappeared. Olivia's will and determination has taken over, her body no longer that of a weak and broken horse. She now has the strength and confidence to carry her through the next few years of living the good life.

Olivia's hardship and story has taught my family a lot about survival, about hope and about people. I often sat and worried about the others, the ones I couldn't save. Sometimes at night when the house is dark and quiet I see their faces. Each time I've witnessed the aftermath of an animal's abuse I'm unable to comprehend how or why it happened. Although I will never understand why anyone felt the need to inflict pain and suffering, I knew there must have been hurt behind their contemptible behavior. Many of these animals survived and ended up in a rescue or sanctuary to recover while others were not as fortunate. Despite difficult and sometimes frightening lives most persevere because of hope and a will to live. But, some are not so lucky. Hope is a powerful thing and yet survival is not possible for many without intervention and the help of others. Small acts of kindness made all the difference for Olivia who's life was hanging by a thread. She is imperfect and what many have called a hay burner. But I call her… a therapist. It may look to some like our horses are without a job, without purpose but that couldn't be further from the truth. Our horses including Olivia bring joy and a peaceful head to all those who have been fortunate enough to have met them. Olivia is loved by many on this farm and blessed to have been rescued and lucky enough to have found her way onto our Fanciful Farm, lucky her... lucky us!

Olivia inspired me and so many others with her fighting spirit and a never-ending will to survive. It makes our daily struggles look small and frivolous. It gives us hope and pride in the people who step up and sacrifice so much to make a difference or to save a life. Things that matter are hard.

Sometimes I wondered how many things had to align themselves in perfect order for Olivia's rescue to have happened. Liv had been spared from the start because she was carrying a foal. She held out before giving birth just long enough to have made it to a safe place under my care. Olivia was so lucky that Cali had learned about the misfortunate horses living on the Appalachian farm and took action. The compassion of my friend who felt compelled to save her life despite the urging of others to put her down was Olivia's saving grace. Thankfully the tender hearts that saw a flame still burning bright in Olivia's eyes followed through despite the sacrifices required.

After the phone call I weighed all the options and almost turned my back as my farm was already full. But then I stopped and thought about how many things must have gone just right for this horse to have knocked on my door. It was too much to deny, so I took a deep breath and didn't worry about how to explain my sudden cross country trip. I guess you could say the stars were aligned for Olivia and she was here today because of it. I don't allow myself to think about what would have happened if Olivia hadn't been rescued. Instead, I think back to where my love of horses began and remembered the day my father led my palomino pony named Stonewall Jackson down the road from a neighboring farm with me riding bareback for the very first time. I still remembered how amazing it felt to sit high upon his back with my legs wrapped around Stoney's belly. I was in love with my first pony and couldn't stop touching and stroking his soft mane. I was so happy that my mouth nearly broke in half from smiling so big. That was a special day and one that remained forever etched in my mind.

This farm has benefited so much by Olivia's rescue. We have learned from her grace and forgiveness. Liv had to learn how to forgive in order to learn to trust us. She had to be willing to let go of what had happened in her past and embrace her new life. She has done this with such ease and gratitude.

In the evenings when I watched the night fall I felt full and complete. I knew my work, although hard and never-ending, was purposeful. As the sun began to droop the big red barn grew quiet. The bees retreated to their colorful box that sweltered with the scent of sweet honey. The chickens retired to the wooden coop to sit out the night on perches next to the barred windows that shielded them from predators that creeped in the night. My cozy settee on the porch of the barn was the perfect place to reflect and rest my tired feet. I sunk into the cushions with the smell of manure at my back as I gazed out over the pond varnished in an evening glow. I took a few deep breaths and closed my eyes for a just a few moments before I finished my evening chores and called it a night. I felt the pressures of farming generations behind me pushing me along. Nightfall seemed far away but it came each night, just as it always had. This barn was much more than a shelter for animals. In the mornings, it was the place where my father and I began our day mucking out stalls while laughing about moments from the past. In the evenings it was there that my husband and I worked side by side and discussed the important parts of our day. On the weekends the concrete in the barn became a dance floor for my granddaughters and sometimes a house of worship and therapy to those who dropped by for an animal fix. This farm, and these animals were my home and my family.

As the crisp air of fall settled, a steady wind picked up and whispered through Olivia's mane. Horses love the coolness after summer has been put to rest. They trot about for no reason at all. Their coats begin to thicken and their middles start to swell while their bodies transitioned to shorter days and frigid temperatures. Even Olivia's coat had grown in the short time she has lived on this farm- masking the scars of her abusive past. Her unorthodox body was less noticeable now. As Olivia put on a few pounds, her bones were less prominent, nestled within. The farm has changed. Just like the leaves on the trees trying on new colors, this farm has welcomed new faces. This farm was and always will be a work in progress with our small herd of special needs animals... something always needs fixing.

As I walked down the woodland path away from my farm I could hear animal sounds at my back. The lovely sounds that brought a farm to life, trailed off in the distance just like a billow of smoke that rose and floated on the horizon before it quietly vanished into thin air. Each turn in life was a step toward the future. It shaped and molded our hearts and our minds in preparation for what was to come. The day I rode my pony down the road to my grandparents farm was a step toward my life today on a farm that was built out of the magic of memories. "Hello little farm"

I suppose my wishing, begging and eventually building this farm brought me face to face with the little girl I knew so well, long ago. I missed the innocent child with soft glowing skin and mousey brown pigtails who seemed to disappear... buried under the weight of adult responsibilities. She has finally returned to the farm and in my mind she is doing barefoot cartwheels in a baby blue and white striped tee shirt that barely met the waistband of her baggy gym shorts; hand-me-downs that every middle child unwillingly tolerated. Perhaps my recreating the best part of my past was a way of bringing back the little girl who ran without worry through the tickle grass behind the old barn with wind licking her long tangled tresses. I see her now standing at arm's length, face to face, the magic that once twinkled in her eyes now melting into the eyes of a middle aged woman in bare feet and wrinkled skin. The outer shell has changed but the gooey center remains the same, soft and savory, relished little by little, each day a little sweeter than the last.

My mouth smiles with the knowledge of my power rekindled. It never left me although it had become invisible for a time. The power to recreate the magic, a life so dear, nestled in the brown soil beneath my feet, glistening in the green leaves that whispered in the breeze and lingering in the breath of fur covered bodies that roamed the pastures, was all MINE. Before my trip to Georgia and before Olivia, I believed that it was luck that brought opportunity to buy the land and build the farm. But now knowing the truth my love has deepened and my life made richer. We make our own luck, our own truths, wants, dreams and wishes- our childlike powers infinite and waiting to come to life.

The day I saved Olivia's life was the day she ultimately saved mine!

Olivia

66

*A promise is a declaration of assurance
that one will do a particular thing or that
a particular thing will happen.*

99

Promises are sometimes made and broken without awareness, without consequences and without regrets. Olivia was alone and frightened before the spy sisters entered her life. Their love and the promise of a better life was given with the best of intentions. But life doesn't always happen exactly the way it is planned.

Olivia felt the breeze wisp through her mane as an unconditional love from four playful hands with dark hair, soft skin and a youthful glow weaved it's way beneath her skin and into her heart. The pungent smell of pine sap and the innocent voices of two young girls surrounding her had brought forth a tearful memory to Olivia's eyes. She felt her past melting into a distant blur with her flesh almost healed and the pain of losing her foal safely tucked away in a corner of her heart. Olivia closed her eyes and enjoyed the chatter of innocent voices. Her mind wandered back to a time when Blondie and Little Red gave her everything a little horse could ever want or need to be whole, happy and loved. Her body tingled in the knowledge that she had somehow made it through many years of danger, uncertainty and pain. She was thankful to be one of the lucky ones who made it out alive.

Her heart felt a little prick as she wondered about her pinto friend. She felt the warmth of his dark chocolate eyes and remembered the moment they melted into hers. Her breath was slow and easy and her mind deep in thought, as her body began to weave with sleepiness until a familiar sound whispered into her ears. It was a voice she had heard many times before and a whinny that made her heart flutter the way it had in the past. Olivia startled and opened her eyes to two achingly beautiful faces, familiar and encompassing of everything Olivia had wished for. Trotting along side the red and blonde little girls was a sight for sore eyes, a pinto in brown and white fur. Olivia blinked and shuttered while she wrestled with her past, their promise, the future and this vision- real or imagined... magic or memory. This sight was magical and almost unimaginable for a little horse who had been through so much in her brief existence. She had seen more than most and had experienced the very worst and the very best in humanity. She opened and closed her eyes several times until her future and her past collided. Olivia blinked again and her eyes came into focus as the red and blonde haired girls melted away to show their true forms. Two brunettes, one with straight hair and one with curls. And her new little pinto friend Chip was running alongside them. The girls called out to Olivia to follow as they ran about giggling through the lush green pasture. Life is sometimes a mystery and often times magical for those who still believe.

Gratitude and Stories

66

Life is fleeting, it turns like a river that ebbs and flows and nothing can stop it's rush to a final spill into deeper waters that erase its time and existence. My wonder leads me to ask; will my time on this river be worth the trip and what will be left of my canoe when I am no longer riding the current?

99

Sometimes when the wind blew just right a memory fell out of the sky and danced before me. The memories from Olivia's rescue were a mixture of pain and healing woven into a layer I still wear today. You can't be part of this type of experience without being changed in some way. Although Olivia's story is sad and the abuse she suffered has left an unforgiving mark on her body, I have chosen instead, to focus on the amazing heroes who made great sacrifices for a little horse we call Olivia. Rescuing has been expensive and draining. It's difficult to become burdened with the problems of others but in the midst of saving something or someone we have ultimately saved ourselves. Although I will never understand why people have abused animals or inflicted misery on others, I have continued to love and help those in need without true understanding.

Being faced with decisions both big and small throughout my lifetime led me to choices made without knowing the full impact on my future or the future of others. When the door opened for Olivia to live on my farm, it also opened the door for me to write this book. Doorways are symbolic concepts that play an important part in our everyday lives. They symbolized change and their openings offer transitions and opportunities. Each character in this book was faced with a dilemma and the opportunity to choose a door to the next phase of their life. I'm so glad I chose Olivia when I took on the challenge of a difficult trip and the lifelong responsibility of keeping her safe. But Olivia had the most difficult choice of all. She closed the door to abuse and neglect from her past and walked through the door that led to forgiveness and trust. This choice is something Olivia had made for herself and we are so very happy she did!

This book is dedicated to all the rescuers who have put themselves out for their fellow human beings or their furry friends. These true heroes are the reason why so many Olivias have received a second chance and a new lease on life. The heroes among us are disguised in many forms and faces. Many rescuers have worked quietly while others have sought the limelight, but they are all important and necessary helpers in this tireless work. Small things, small deeds have made a difference to those who are desperate. Even the little turtle who was helped across the road before a passing vehicle could take his life is an example of such random acts of kindness shown by everyday heroes like yourself.

The world of rescue is not for the faint of heart, it's filled with a lot of hard work and self-sacrifice. Rescuers are not your average people, they are individuals with a passion and a heart of gold. These heroes that walk among us carry out their passions with an animal in need planted in their heart. These brave missionaries were quite often misunderstood and many times asked, "Why do you do it?"

The community of rescuers is a tight-knit group who work together to make the world a better place. Someone once said, "Many hearts beating together makes us stronger."

There are many Olivias out there and I would like to share a few stories from some of our fellow rescuers. Their words are important and their hearts are golden. The beauty that matters most in this life is not on the outside... It is the sacrifice made and time given away to help a struggling soul survive.

Here are their stories...

Danielle Raad of Fanciful Farming said,

I received a text message one September day with a picture and the words "she needs us, are you up for a road trip?" I didn't even have to question where the text had come from... I knew it was from my mother. This wasn't the first time I had received this type of question. We had already rescued 3 other horses within that same year along with an unwanted bunny and a few misfit chickens. Many of which were out of state and required long hours in the car to retrieve them. I HATE road trips, I get motion sickness easily. I prefer my trips in the comfort of an airplane. But I agreed anyways to travel all the way to Georgia with my mother.

Most would say my mother was crazy for doing this... yet again. So I guess that makes me crazy for going along with it. That's ok, at least I'm not boring!

Rescuing animals became second nature for me since the day I saved that tiny monarch caterpillar in the rain storm. It had sparked a motivation in me in a way that I hadn't ever been motivated before. I began utilizing the farm surroundings to nurture hundreds of tiny caterpillars until they were ready to emerge as monarch butterflies. The property that the farm sits on is a tantalizing and stunning piece of land. Surrounded by newer home developments, the 36 acres almost feels like an oasis but long ago it had been a large cattle pasture. The farm originally was our town's most lucrative family owned business as a dairy farm producing and selling ice cream. The dairy's farmhouse still proudly stands to this day as a Historical Landmark, evolved into a museum for tourists and school groups. Even though it's been many years since it was a cattle pasture, when it rains it still smells of fresh cow manure, giving us subtle hints into the past. I love that smell...

After the property changed hands, it was bought by a local horticulturist who treasured the land. He spent many years planting oak, dogwood, white pine and sassafras trees. Along with berry shrubs, milkweed and wildflowers. I remember as a child seeing him out working the land in his denim overalls and large straw hat.

In the summer months it is frequented by many woodland animals and birds that come to fish from the ponds. Eagles soar above, tree frogs chorus and does graze with their fawns. Antique rusted horseshoes, corked glass medicine bottles, green glass fence insulators and even Native American artifacts have been dug from this rich earth. It is a place of sanctuary and healing. You can feel it's spirit while you walk down it's many winding paths. I knew that bringing Olivia here would help her heal emotionally and physically as it has healed the others.. as it has healed me.

When I first met Olivia I was a bit startled by her incredibly odd gait. I cringed as I watched her move. It looked odd and painful. I knelt down to be at her eye level. She tightened up as I touched her chest. I could feel scars under her hair and she was incredibly thin but her eyes still had a sparkle to them.

At the family farm I mostly "specialize" in the care of the honey bees, monarchs and chickens. Chickens can be challenging at times but I feel they are very misunderstood creatures who often get overlooked for their contributions and sacrifices, so I try my very best to provide a long and happy life to the lucky ones that get to call this farm home.

I didn't grow up with horses. Owning horses didn't come until my two daughters were gifted a pair of two pinto mini horses (Cowboy and Flynn) at the young ages of 2 and 4 years old. I immediately fell in love with their mysterious spirits and silent language. I have learned the care and challenges of horses through my mother and rescuing has become natural for us and expected. When I met Olivia that day in Georgia I could sense her strong spirit and could see she still had a will to live. She had a purpose…

that blue eye had a story that needed to be told.

Danielle Raad is my daughter and Fanciful Farms rescue partner.

• • ◉ ◉ ◉ ◉ • •

Mindy of Whiskey Acres said,

The morning of January 21, 2017 changed my life as a rescuer forever. I was sworn in by our county as a Humane Police Officer just a week prior to the call coming in on that cold January morning. I received a complaint about a horse that was being severely neglected. I gathered all of the information and pictures, called the State Police for backup, and drove out to the location. What we found was just horrifying. Here stands a Shetland pony in mud up to his knees, no food or water, and a very disfigured mouth. The owner admitted to a family member hitting "Whiskey" in the mouth with a shovel 10 years prior. No veterinary treatment was rendered in the 10 years. He lived off of grain soaked in water; which is what he still thrives on today. The owner surrendered Whiskey to our rescue and the very stressful and undetermined future for Whiskey began. Every veterinarian and equine dentist immediately recommended euthanasia as they have never seen anything like this in their careers. "This pony shouldn't be alive" is a phrase I heard over and over. But we saw Whiskey's spirit and just couldn't give up on him that easily. We consulted with Ohio State University and they agreed to assess him. We made the 4 hour drive and the news we received there was not good. They had never seen anything like what this pony had endured. It was determined that his teeth were growing into his sinus cavity, he had shear mouth, lock jaw, and would need to have his occipital bone removed in order to open his mouth.

The removal of this bone lead to a discussion on what the end result may be, euthanasia, blindness, deafness, etc. OSU gave him a less than 10% chance of survival. We were willing to take that chance. The following day, the staff of 11 doctors and assistants came out to reveal that everything was a success! We are very pleased to announce that Whiskey is now a case study for OSU and that he is thriving here at "Whiskey Acres Sanctuary" with the same love and spirit as he did the first day we rescued him. We never gave up on Whiskey and he has changed our lives forever. To learn more about Whiskey, please check him out on Facebook at Whiskey Miracle Pony and/or Whiskey Acres Sanctuary or visit our website at: www.whiskeyacressanctuary.org.

Mindy James, VP, Whiskey Acres Sanctuary

. . . ● . ● . .

Jodi of Saved by Zade said,

In 2014 a pregnant black cat showed up on our doorstep. It was the beginning of home schooling for my chronically ill daughter. Between the black cat's eyes and my daughters eyes I could tell she was going to stay. She had her kittens that night and we quickly learned how to bottle feed them because there were too many kittens for one mama to feed.

As the years went on, people contacted me on a regular basis (over seventy in one week) to bottle feed baby kittens. My daughter thought she wanted to be a veterinarian and because she was homeschooled we had the opportunity to do something unique to get her into college. So we started a nonprofit rescue to help kitties.

I just want to say I am personally allergic to cats!

Jodi of Saved by Zade

• • • ● ● ● ● • •

Toni of Lifting Spirits said,

While growing up I was always rescuing animals, whether it was from the local barn, injured off the streets or dumped in a field. I would either bring them home or to the local animal hospital. They were helpless, scared and some didn't make it. I will never forget the look in their eyes, it always tore at my heart and I knew I needed to do something no matter what situation they were in.

I realized early on that horses were my spirit animal. My whole life I've thought they were amazing, magical and beautiful. I could connect and bond with them. They were always there for me during good and bad times. They never judged or complained and I always felt healed by them.

After college and children, my work slowed down and I decided to take my career on a different path. I needed horses back in my life and I finally had the finances and time to do that. That is when I decided to start my nonprofit. Seeing so many unwanted horses on social media, in the news, at auctions, and on craigslist made me decide to save them. I feel that all my horses found me and were placed into my life for a reason by a higher power. Every horse that I have rescued and saved has been an amazing gift. And I know God can only give me what I can handle.

All my rescues whether a dog, cat, or horse, have taught me so much. Even though they all had different stories and came from all over the country, they all have one thing in common and that is a kind soul. They all know they were rescued, are being loved and cared for, so in return, they have given this all back to me and more. And this is what fills my heart and soul.

These are just some examples of what I have experienced and learned while rescuing each animal: sadness, joy, anger(that they were put into this position,) saving a life, giving a second chance, unconditional love, the unknown, taking a risk, giving up to a higher power, loving so much your heart aches, bonding, soul mates, giving back, helping others, following your gut instinct, determined, worried about finances, patience, sharing, letting go, making a difference, making new friends and supporting other rescues.

I am not sure what makes the human species treat animals in this way, I will never understand it but can only try and help fix it. Even if it is just one animal at a time. I will never stop rescuing or supporting others like myself, it is in my blood and God bless all others who rescue these animals that need to be saved.

Toni Hadad, President/Founder

Lifting Spirits Miniature Therapy Horses

• • • ◉ ◉ • • •

Louise of Wildside said,

It all started when I was 8. The baby bird or the baby squirrel that fell from their nest and ended up in my care. No veterinarian knew about wildlife care, nor was I ever referred to a wildlife rehabilitator. I just did the best I could with the help of my mom and a friend's mom who was in this with me. This was my first experience of what it was like to be a wildlife rehabilitator.

Fast forward 20 years.... A wildlife center in my area was looking for volunteers. Within a few visits, I was hooked. NOW, I could really help. NOW, I was learning how to save the lives of the baby birds and squirrels. I quickly became the volunteer coordinator and eventually assistant director of the center. I lived on the premises and took care of thousands of wild animals while I was there.

In 1995, after leaving the center at which I had spent 5 years, I opened Wildside Rehabilitation and Education Center in Eaton Rapids, MI. Wildside specializes in caring for injured, orphaned and ill native MI wildlife and sharing knowledge with the public so we can all co-exist together in this world. I now have the skills and knowledge to care for hundreds of wild animals per year with the help of about 40 volunteers, local veterinarians and of course, still, my mom. Now, I am a wildlife rehabilitator.

Louise Sagaert, Wildside Director

• • • ● ● ● • •

Danielle from Hot off the Nest said,

Dayton's timing for making her way to me was so very perfect looking back. I received a text from my mom one day in late March that someone had found a stray chicken wandering in downtown Dayton, Ohio and it needed a home and she wondered if I could take her in. I nearly said no, I had a lot on my plate as my now ex-husband was in the process of moving out of our home. I even remember starting to type back "no, I really can't take anything else on right now" only to delete it and just simply respond "yes".

Dayton was delivered to me two days later- she was dirty, almost half her feathers were broken off, she was very thin (barely over a pound) and was the most completely and utterly scared bird I had ever met. I could barely even get her out of the crate they brought her in.

She had been found running in a busy street downtown and I'd imagine she'd either "fallen off the truck" leaving a mass production egg laying farm or something of the like. She appeared to be a white leghorn, her comb was enormous, her beak clipped and she had long, stained nails - all signs pointing to her being a battery hen.

I quickly learned she got overstimulated by the smallest of things. I had to cover her kennel with a sheet, all except for one side because she'd jump and bang into the cage sides if anybody or anything approached her too quickly. I would change her food and water by moving as slowly as I possibly could and she'd still get upset.

Many a day I would just spend sitting in front of her cage talking about nothing just to let her hear my voice. I'd feed Crossley, my crossbeak hen, in front of her. I'd sit closer and closer to her pen everyday. Ever so painstakingly slowly, Dayton settled in. She stopped jumping at every movement and she started eating in front of me. Soon I could touch her, then pick her up, then all the sudden she like basically ruled my house and claimed the back of my couch by a large window during the day and a certain wing back chair as her roost spot at night.

I have since rescued 4 more battery hens as Dayton's "sisters" and they all live outside now with my bantam flock. They are some of the most sassy, excited birds in my flock - I can't believe how unfazed they are by their previous lives. They've quite literally shed every little flake of their time as battery hens and act as if they have never not been here, scratching around in the grass and soaking up the sunshine.

Everyone is always commenting on my Instagram about how much Dayton has blossomed in my care, but I think the truth is we both bloomed together. Dayton needed someone with patience and time and I needed something else to focus on when I was going through some big shifts in my life. Even when I'd have a bad day, I'd walk by her and see this little bird who had been shoved in a tiny, itty cage most of her life who still somehow had a sparkle in her eye and a perk in her peck and all of the sudden things felt a little less grim. The pretty little leghorn with a personality as big as her floppy comb kept me smiling through it all.

Some rescues you seek out, and some just find you. Some are only with us for a few hours, some we get to enjoy their company for years. Sometimes you need them just as much as they need you!

Danielle Noll owner/curator of Hot Off the Nest on Instagram and Facebook

Thank you!

"

> *My life embraced by time, an open doorway and the path I have chosen.*

"

B eing thankful and expressing my gratitude is an important part of my happiness. I would like to end Saving Olivia with my gratitude for the writing contributions given by friends who shared their hearts and stories with me. I am also thankful and hold great admiration for the girls who risked their lives during the first rescue of Olivia. I would especially like to thank my husband for the many years of happy marriage and for his constant love and support of all of my dreams and destinations. Thank you to my parents for loving and allowing me to become the free spirit I was destined to be. To my daughter who shares my passion for rescue, thank you for your beautiful contributions to this book. She wrote a beautiful prologue, giving wings to my story. To my sons, my daughter, my husband and grandchildren, thank you for making my life worth living. I owe a huge and overwhelming thank you to my sister and daughter who encouraged me, and kept my writing on track during the many hours of editing- I couldn't have done it without you. And lastly, a big thank you to the many friends and supporters of our Fanciful Farm.

Olivia's story continues on Facebook and Instagram. If you would like to learn more about Olivia and the farm that she lives on today please visit **Fanciful Farming** on Facebook and Instagram.

· · · ● ● ● · ·

The End

66

Now this is not the end. It is not even the beginning of the end. But it is, perhaps, the end of the beginning. -Winston Churchill

99

Olivia soon after being rescued